MEANT FOR EACH OTHER
Lee Duran

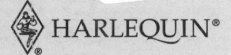

HARLEQUIN®

TORONTO • NEW YORK • LONDON
AMSTERDAM • PARIS • SYDNEY • HAMBURG
STOCKHOLM • ATHENS • TOKYO • MILAN • MADRID
PRAGUE • WARSAW • BUDAPEST • AUCKLAND

ISBN-13: 978-0-373-71535-0
ISBN-10:   0-373-71535-8

MEANT FOR EACH OTHER

www.eHarlequin.com

Printed in U.S.A.

ABOUT THE AUTHOR

Some people climb mountains because they're there. Lee Duran writes books because blank sheets of paper make her nervous when there's always another story that needs to be told. She currently lives in Colorado or Missouri or both, or in between, depending. She shares her abode with a Maltese named Spike and a massive mostly Bouvier ninety-pounder named Jackie O.

CHAPTER ONE

THE TELEPHONE shrilled in the middle of the night and Frankie reacted as mothers and grandmothers do the world over: she bolted upright in bed, her heart pounding and her breathing shallow. The phone rang again, the sound terrifying in the dark bedroom, piercing and urgent. She stumbled out of bed and shuffled toward the table next to her reading chair, stubbing her toe in the process.

"Hello?"

"Mrs. Davis?"

"I, uh, I used to be. Yes, I'm Mrs. Davis. What—"

"It's your husband, ma'am."

"Ex-husband."

"Well, your name and phone number is the only one he carried. This is Memorial Hospital in St. Louis. Mr. Davis was just brought in by ambulance and—"

"Oh, my God!" Frankie sat down hard in the chair next to the phone table. "What happened?"

"A car accident—he ran into a tree. The weather's impossible and getting worse. Mr. Davis rolled his car on the icy roads."

"In St. Louis? He lives in Ch-Chicago. What—" Her mind struggled to make sense of all this. Did anything good ever begin with a middle-of-the-night phone call?

"Mrs. Davis," the disembodied voice interrupted, "we're not sure yet what happened, but as next of kin—"

"M-me?" The chilly temperature of the room seemed to sink right into her bones, and she began to shiver uncontrollably.

"If you could come—"

"I don't think he'd want to see me if I did."

"Is there anyone else we can notify? Parents, children—"

"Not our children. They're in no position to drop everything and go to him. They live too far away."

A silence, and then the woman said, "Mrs. Davis, I don't think you understand what's happened. Mr. Davis is in a coma and in extremely serious shape. If there is anyone who cares about this man—"

"I care." Frankie choked out the words, deeply offended by the woman's insinuation. "I'll have to drive— airports shut down yesterday. I'm at least two hours away from the closest one anyway, and that's in good weather. As soon as this ice storm calms down, I'll drive."

"Very well. But I must stress, his condition is serious."

"Are you telling me he might d-die?"

"That's always that possibility in cases such as this. Of course, we're doing all we can."

"What are his injuries?"

"Broken bones, a concussion… There's a chance he suffered a heart attack, which could help explain the accident, but at this point we can't be sure."

A heart attack. Oh, God.

"Are you there, Mrs. Davis?"

"Yes, I'm sorry." She shook herself out of her sorrow. "I'll be there as soon as I can. If he wakes up, please don't tell him that I'm coming."

"I'll put a note on his chart about your wishes."

"Thank you. I'll wait until daylight to leave. I don't know how long it will take me to get there, due to road conditions."

Mission accomplished, the woman softened. "Drive carefully," she said. "It's awful out there. In the meantime, I'll give you the phone number here at the nurses' station in intensive care, and the address of the hospital. Do you have a pencil?"

"No, but give me a minute." Frankie turned on the light, blinked in the glare, then snatched up a pen. "I'm ready…"

Or maybe not, she thought, taking notes.

WITH SLEEP OUT of the question, Frankie threw a few things into a suitcase. She'd have to go by the café first and wait for Lynda to arrive for work to brief her on the situation, then call one or the other of her daughters. Secure in the car, she raised the garage door and backed out into a frenzy of frozen rain and darkness.

Heart in her throat, she turned on the windshield wipers and crept into the street. Visibility terrible even with the wipers at full tilt, she drove—or rather slipped and slid—to the front door of Reva's Café. For a frightening moment Frankie thought the car would slide right through the front door, but at the last minute the tires found traction.

Sleet and freezing rain continued to slam against the vehicle, and Frankie slumped over the steering wheel. She hadn't recovered from the shock and still felt weak and panicky. How the hell was she supposed to get to St. Louis in weather like this? It was a dumb idea. St. Louis was clear across the state. She'd be an idiot even to try.

But she had to try. Even if Johnny refused to see her, she couldn't leave him alone on the edge of death. *I'm a good driver,* she assured herself, trying to relax. *I've lived through other ice storms and I'll live through this one. I can do this.*

I can *do this.*

She couldn't bear to think of Johnny being alone in a strange city, in a strange hospital, perhaps dying or already…she caught her breath…dead. Tears threatened at the thought. She'd married the man three times and divorced him three times, but she would love him until the day she died. If only he'd been faithful. If only she'd been smart. If only he'd been honest. If only she'd been strong.

Crappy words, *if only.* All that was done and gone. The present was risky enough so she wouldn't think of what had been.

She threw herself out of the car and dashed to the front door of the café she'd inherited from her mother. Wet and cold, it took Frankie a long time to fumble the key into the lock and shove open the door. A flick of a switch flooded the room with light and she stepped inside, out of reach of the elements.

Reva's, an old-time diner of red vinyl and yellowed posters, had been a landmark here in Fairweather, Missouri, for decades. Opened in the 1940s by Grandma Reva Brown, it had been passed on to her daughter Mary Ann Brown Hale and then to Frankie Hale Davis. Popularity never wavered for the only decent place to eat in the small community.

Like her mother, Frankie took care to maintain the original ambience of the place. She kept the same heavy china mugs and dinnerware, the same blah-type linoleum on the floor, the posters of Roy Acuff and Eddie Arnold, the original sign that warned diners that only those wearing shoes and shirts would be served.

Fortunately the sign did not attempt to anticipate what was to come in fashion. Reva would never have condoned hot pants, for example, but Mary and Frankie were ready to bend to clothing trends…to a point.

The clock above the cashier's station declared it to be 3:47 a.m. Lynda should arrive soon to get ready for the 5:00 a.m. opening, assuming she could get here at all. In the meantime, Frankie might as well make herself useful. She didn't dare leave before dawn, nor would she call her daughters at this hour.

A pot of coffee was always the first order of business since turning on the lights meant the restaurant was open. Behind the counter, she filled the glass container with fresh cold water, then scooped in coffee grounds. The sound of the door opening sent her spinning around, surprise making her heart pound all over again.

Ron Baker stood there, shaking water and ice off his coat and hair like a big shaggy dog. "Brr." He threw off the jacket and it landed on the backrest of a booth before slicing onto the floor. "Was I ever glad to see your light when I came around the bend. What you doing here at this hour, girl?"

Frankie hadn't been a girl in years, but she didn't correct him. "Waiting to see if Lynda's going to make it in to open up this morning. What's your excuse?"

"I just hauled Ray Benjamin's ass out of a ditch south of here. Got my towing rig outside." He gestured with a shoulder toward the parking lot before ambling to the counter and swinging onto a stool. "Sure could use a cuppa joe."

"It'll be ready in a few minutes." She dried her hands on a nearby towel. "Been a busy night?"

"I'll say. If people don't get off these roads, some damn fool is gonna kill hisself sure." He looked at her with a hopeful expression on his broad, friendly face. "I don't suppose you could scare up a coupla' eggs and maybe a slice of ham back there, could you? I had a bologna sandwich for supper and ate the damned thing in the cab of my truck."

"I think I can find something," Frankie said, teasing him. She'd known Ron all her life, as she did most of the residents of this little town tucked in at the south-western edge of the Missouri Ozarks. He was one of the good guys. So was his wife, Myrna.

Frankie turned to the refrigerator and started pulling out what she'd need. Behind her, Ron shifted on his stool.

"Looks like we're about to have more company," he said.

"Who—"

She turned just in time to see the door fly open and a bundled figure stumble inside. A knit hat flew one way, a long fringed scarf another, and Brenda Frazier emerged, her round, middle-aged face scrunched up and red from the cold.

Frankie shook her head in disbelief. "Brenda, what in the world are you doing out in this weather at this time of night?"

"I just got off work, believe it or not. I was supposed to finish my shift at eleven, but we had a couple of emergencies because of some highway pileup north of here. I hung around to help Doc out."

She struggled out of her heavy coat and hung it

neatly on a hook near the door. "Was I ever glad to see your lights. I don't think I could have made it home, what with all the slipping and sliding."

Rubbing her hands together to warm them, Brenda joined Ron at the counter. Cheeks rosy as Santa's, she looked hopefully at the burbling coffeepot.

"I'd kill for a cup of coffee," she announced.

Frankie reached for cups. "I don't believe this. I thought I'd be here all alone."

Brenda cocked her head. "Now that you mention it, what are *you* doing here at this hour?"

Before Frankie could reply, the door slammed open again and Lynda barged in, her face pale and grim.

"I sideswiped a stop sign on Main Street and had to walk here," she said, struggling out of her coat and scarf. "I've seen an ice storm or two in my day, but this is a mother."

"I wasn't sure you'd make it today," Frankie said. "I intended to call you but—"

"Couldn't have. Phone lines are down." Brenda nodded at the newcomer. "Hi, Lynda. Glad you made it in, weather considered."

"And how." Lynda rubbed her hands together. "We're lucky we got electricity here, let alone phones." She glanced at Ron. "You're an early riser."

"Haven't been to bed yet."

"Bummer." Lynda grabbed a fresh apron from a hook behind the counter. "Thanks for opening for me," she said to Frankie.

Brenda leaned back on her stool. "Frankie was just about to tell us why she's here at this hour. You came in and got us off the subject."

"She came to open up," Lynda said reasonably.

Brenda looked skeptical. "I don't think so. Frankie?"

"Well…I didn't actually come in just to open up. I needed to talk to you, Lynda."

Lynda paused expectantly, hands on her apron strings.

Frankie licked her dry lips, less than eager to share her business with curious onlookers. She sighed. They'd know soon enough anyway. Gossip had a life of its own in this town.

"I have to go to St. Louis," she said, "and I didn't want to leave until morning, what with the roads the way they are. I've still got to call Katy, too, if the phones come back on. I didn't want to wake her up too early and scare her."

"You're gonna drive in this?" Ron looked horrified.

Brenda spoke first. "If you call Katy and Laura and tell them you're going out in this, it will scare them shitless, no matter what time of day it is. What are you thinking?"

"Trust me on this," Ron put in. "The weather's going no place but downhill. It ain't a fit day out for man nor beast."

Lynda added, "What earthly reason would send you on a trip like that today?"

"It's Johnny," Frankie said. "He needs me, whether he knows it or not."

The waitress frowned. "You haven't seen that guy in months, that I know of. Why are you doing this? You've been divorced for years."

"Have you two made up?" Brenda leaned forward on her stool, her eyes bright and hopeful.

Ron chuckled. "I'll bet that's it. I knew it was only a matter of time before you two did what you do best—marry each other one more time. I think it's kind of like going to Disneyland every few years, just to see if it's changed."

Brenda and Lynda laughed. Frankie didn't.

"He's been in an accident in St. Louis," she said. "Do you expect me to sit here and wait to hear what's going on when he's there all alone, in a coma?"

She'd really slapped it to them and they all looked appalled by their previous comments.

"Ah, hell." Ron's shoulders slumped. "What happened? Car wreck?"

"He hit a tree, so they tell me. They're not yet sure how much damage was done."

"Nevertheless," Brenda said gently, "you can't take this chance. Wait until the weather's better."

"I can't do that. There isn't time." Frankie opened an egg carton. "Want a couple of eggs while I'm at it, Brenda?"

"Yeah, I guess so. Frankie, it's too dangerous to try driving clear across the state of Missouri. I'd do anything for Johnny, and most in this town would, but you've got to remember that you're not married to him anymore. There's no need to risk your life."

"That's not the way I see it."

"You won't make it to Joplin," Ron predicted. "I just hope you slide into a ditch—a real shallow ditch—before you reach the Fairweather city limits sign. Then I can haul you home and lock you in."

Lynda added, "It won't do Johnny any good if you kill yourself on the way."

"I won't. I'm a good driver. I can do this."

"I don't think a NASCAR driver could do it on those roads," Ron said.

"I'll be careful. I'll drive slow."

"And whatcha gonna do about all the *bad* drivers hogging the roads? It'll take a miracle for you to get through to St. Louis in one piece."

"I believe in miracles," Frankie said softly. "I have to."

Lynda let out a gust of breath. "Then I'll believe, too. There's something special about you and Johnny, even considering all your ups and downs. I'll just say a prayer and wish you well."

"Thanks, Lynda. I knew I could count on you."

Frankie turned back to the grill where breakfast sizzled, gritting her teeth against her emotions. Reaching for the spatula, she heard Brenda telling Ron the latest.

"You hear about that Cannon girl who ran away from home a couple of days ago? I understand they caught her in the mall in Joplin with a walletful of her mother's credit cards."

"Hadn't heard they caught her," Ron said. "I do know her folks have spoiled that girl rotten. The day before she took off, she dumped her lunch tray on top of the cash register at the school cafeteria. I hear she got suspended."

"That's not exactly the way I heard it…."

Idle gossip. Frankie didn't even want to listen. If anyone knew what gossip could do, it was Frankie Hale Davis.

Lynda came up beside her. "Here, let me take over the grill. The phones are working again so you better make your calls before they go down again."

"Thanks, Lynda." She gave the woman a quick hug

and turned away, her heart beating skittishly and her palms clammy. Time to call Katy and then…the road awaited.

"KATY, HONEY, IT'S MOM."

"Mom?" She sounded groggy and disoriented. "What's wrong?"

"It's your father."

"Daddy?" A scared alertness entered her tone. "What is it?"

Frankie filled her in quickly and added, "Now don't get all hysterical on me. Have a little faith. Your father's tough. He'll get through this."

Katy drew a quick breath but when she spoke, her voice still sounded wobbly. "You're right, there's no point in falling apart. But Daddy…I just can't believe it."

Katy and her sister, Laura, had always adored their father. Frankie understood about girls and fathers. She'd had a father of her own, once. Most of the time, she'd loved and trusted him.

"I can't believe it, either. Listen, I need you to let your sister know what's happened. I don't feel up to going through this again."

"Of course, but…"

"Tell her I'm heading to St. Louis as quick as I can get there."

"Oh, Mom, with the roads the way they are— Why are you doing this? Things haven't been too great between you and Dad lately."

"That's not exactly the case. Yes, we've had our problems but I will love your father until the day I die. He needs me there and I'm going."

Katy let out an exasperated sigh. "I don't understand you two and I never will. I guess you're all grown up, though, and I can't stop you."

"That's exactly right. Don't worry, Katy. I'm sure the weather's worse in Arkansas than it is here," Frankie lied as convincingly as she could.

"But—"

"I'll be leaving in a few minutes, and I don't want you girls to worry, not about either of us. I'll call as soon as I get there and find out how your father is."

"But—"

"No time, sugar. I'm going to keep my cell phone off unless I need to make a call, because I didn't think to grab the charger. Bye-bye. Kiss the kids for Grandma."

Frankie hung up, then leaned her forehead against the wall next to the phone. It was time to go and she was scared—she could lie to everyone else about that but not herself. She'd be all right after a few miles.

"Hey, Frankie!"

She turned. Ron stood just inside the door, his smiling wife, Myrna, beside him.

"What are you doing back here?" Frankie asked. "Wasn't your first breakfast enough?"

Ron grinned. He tossed a key chain into the air and caught it, metal jingling.

"What?"

The two of them wound their way across the room toward her. When they got close enough, he flipped Frankie the key ring.

"What's this?" She frowned down at the keys in her hand.

"Keys to my Jeep," Myrna said, beaming. "Ron

says that light little car of yours wouldn't make it to Springfield."

"Maybe the Jeep won't, either," Ron put in, "but if worse comes to worst it'll give you better protection."

"Oh, Myrna, I can't take your new car."

"The hell you can't." Ron looked from one woman to the other. "It was her idea, Frankie. A'course, I was gonna take the keys away from her anyway." He gave Frankie an "I'm kidding" wink and nudged Myrna with his elbow.

"But what if I wreck it or sideswipe a tree or something?" Frankie said.

"It's insured," Myrna said.

"Take the damn car," Ron pushed.

"You two…" Frankie shook her head in wonder. "What can I say?" Her eyes threatened to tear up again but she blinked away the moisture. Frankie was not a crybaby. Usually. Maybe she had been in her youth but not these days.

"You could say you've changed your mind and are gonna stay home till this melts off," Ron suggested.

"Can't do it."

"Then I'll lead you to the city limits in the tow truck to make sure you get there."

"In that case—" Frankie stepped up and gave him a strong hug, which he returned. The second hug went to Myrna.

"We all love you, Frankie," he said gruffly, "and that fellow of yours, for that matter. Did you know he backed me when I went into the towing business? He's a silent partner, I guess you could say. I'd never have been able to swing it without him."

"I didn't know, but I'm not surprised."

"We all want you both back here safe and sound," Myrna chimed in. "Don't forget that."

"I won't," she promised. But what she thought was *I'll be back but I can't speak for Johnny.*

FRANKIE DIDN'T LIKE driving strange vehicles but she had to admit, Myrna's red Jeep handled a lot better than her own small car. Not that she fooled herself into believing that *any* vehicle was safe on a solid sheet of ice. She might be determined but she wasn't stupid.

She followed Ron to the edge of town, moving cautiously through the gloomy morning. The sleet had slowed, or so she thought, and she took that as a good sign. Once she got to Joplin and hit the highway east, she'd be fine.

Ron pulled carefully into the parking lot of the Grab and Gulp Liquor Store just inches outside the city limits. Rolling down his window, he waved her on and she crept slowly past. She was on her own now. No traffic in sight, not a bird or a squirrel to be seen.

I wish Johnny were here, she thought, trying to flex the taut muscles of her arms. It seemed as if he always appeared when she needed him…. Of course, if he were here and fine, she'd be safe at home, wondering what he might be doing.

TRAFFIC INCREASED as Frankie neared Joplin, and for a time she stopped thinking about anything but the road. The sleet continued, although it wasn't as thick, which improved visibility a bit. Once she got on Highway 44 heading toward Springfield, she breathed a sign of relief and became aware of the painful tension in her shoulders, and down her arms and in her wrists and fingers.

She needed to stop, walk around a bit, try to relax. A drive that should take thirty minutes had instead taken more than two hours, and she felt every tension-packed minute of it.

All for Johnny. As she drove, searing memories flooded back....

CHAPTER TWO

1963

I GREW UP IN a little bitty Missouri town perched on the side of a hill in what my mother always called "the foothills of the Ozarks." I knew everyone in town and everyone knew me—"You're Mike Hale's only girl," they'd say, as if telling me something I didn't know.

Fairweather was actually an awful name for this little town in the "Show Me" state. If there was one thing we didn't have it was fair weather. Like the rest of the state, it was either too cold or too hot with the kind of humidity that wilted the unwary.

Still, the town ran on a schedule that shaped my life: school, of course; the big Fourth of July celebration; the little August rodeo where all the locals got to strut around and show off their dubious cowboy skills; the community-wide Christmas celebration; and the Easter sunrise service all marked my growing-up years.

Most of all, I looked forward with great anticipation to the Fourth of July celebration in my sixteenth summer. As incoming president of the Future Homemakers of America, I was responsible for our booth at the big community commemoration near the bandstand at Myrtle Jensen Park. The whole town turned out every year for speeches and concerts and lots of good food, plus carnival rides and games for the kids.

Of course, I made my famous—at least in this town—red, white and blue frosted sugar cookies to sell at the Future Homemakers booth. Mom taught me how to bake and she was the owner and "chef" of Reva's Café. No one disputed that she was the best cook around, now that Grandma, who gave the café her name, was gone.

Excited and happy, I dressed for the day in the new cotton sundress I'd made just for this occasion: navy-blue gingham checks with red trim and a full skirt. I'd even slept in fat curlers the night before, something I rarely did because "sleep" wasn't easy to come by with rolls the size of miniature tomato soup cans pinned to my head. It was worth it, though. When I pulled my normally stick-straight brown hair back into a ponytail it curved down my back in one smooth, beautiful curl.

I looked nice. I'd never be pretty like my friend Joanie, or smart like Carrie, but they couldn't cook like me. Nor did they know one end of a sewing machine from the other. To each her own.

I was satisfied and happy that day, and filled with anticipation.

Mom called from the front door of our house. "Grab that carton of cookies and let's go. I've still got to load up the wiener truck and get it to the park."

"Coming, Mom." But first, I looked in the mirror and said my daily affirmation: *I believe something wonderful will happen to me today.*

It rarely did, but there was nothing wrong in thinking positive.

JOANIE SIDLED UP and whispered in my ear. "That new guy over by the bandstand is as cute as… I swear, he's cute as can be!"

His back was to us and I couldn't see a thing. "You should know, Joanie," I said. "When it comes to cute guys, you're the town expert."

It was easy to see why. Her blond hair cascaded around her face and to her shoulders, over the spaghetti straps of her flowered sundress, which had been bought, not made, I noticed. She made a face at me, and even that was cute.

Joanie was so cute and popular that she'd dated every good-looking guy at Fairweather High School, and some of the smart ones, too. On top of that, she was *nice.* She'd also been one of my two best friends since first grade.

I offered her a cookie, and instead of tasting it, she held it in her hand. "Is this cute guy next on your list?" I asked.

She rolled her eyes and sighed longingly. "I sure hope so. He's from Chicago and his dad has big bucks. His parents are separated and his mom moved here to get away from big-city problems, whatever that means. He got his own car on his sixteenth birthday and he plays baseball and—"

"How the heck did you find all this out?"

She shrugged. "A girl has to keep her ears open."

I had to laugh at that. Everybody in this town kept their ears open.

"You're good at that," I said, "except in algebra class. Still seems strange to me, though. After living in Chicago, I'm surprised they even knew how to find this wide spot in the road."

"She's from here."

"His mom?" I glanced around but saw no one who struck me as out of place or unfamiliar. "Don't go too crazy over this boy, Joanie. They won't stick it out here for long, you mark my words."

"Then I'd better make hay while the sun shines!" Laughing, she tossed the unbitten cookie into the trash can and if she hadn't taken off like a flash, I'd have smacked her for that.

THE FIRST BATCH of cookies sold out, and I hastened to fetch more from Mom's car. I skipped over the ground, feeling light and excited and completely in the holiday spirit.

Hoisting out the last large carton of cookies into my arms, I turned away from the car so suddenly that the box slammed into someone or something. I staggered and the box slipped.

"I got it!"

The weight of my burden suddenly lessened and I found myself staring up into the face of the best-looking boy I ever saw in my life. I think my jaw dropped. I think my eyes must have been as big as dinner plates. I think I realized in that first instant that Joanie had hit it right on the button this time.

"I'm Johnny Davis," he introduced himself in a deep, clear voice, "and you're Frankie Hale."

"H-how did you know?" I couldn't seem to catch my breath beneath his gaze.

"My mother went to school with your mother." He nodded toward Mom's wiener truck, set up at the edge of a grassy area. Sure enough, a woman I'd never seen before spoke animatedly with Mom. She was wearing high heels and high hair—boy, did his mother stand out among the casual dressers.

"She was Dorothy Simpson then."

"Oh, I know some Simpsons," I said, my heart still pounding away. Somehow I couldn't make myself quit staring at him.

Johnny shifted the box to one hip. "We just moved here from Chicago. I'm real happy to meet you, Frankie. Uh…where do you want this box?"

"The Future Homemakers booth." I pointed to the banner marking our territory, then walked beside him. "Will you be going to school here?"

"Yes."

"Senior?"

"That's right."

"Me, too." *Oh, goody!*

He set the box on the counter and turned to me with a smile. My God, his eyes were as blue as the sky and framed by long, dark lashes. Dimples creased his tanned cheeks. I was instantly smitten—or more accurately, I'd been instantly smitten.

"Anything else I can do for you?"

"You can eat a few cookies as your reward," I said, thinking fast to keep him here.

"Glad to." He opened the flaps of the box and peered inside. "Did you make these?"

"Yes." I said it proudly. "Try one. Or take two. They're small."

They weren't small, they were huge, but he didn't argue. He took a bite. I waited anxiously, although I don't know why. I was a great baker. Still…I wanted him to approve.

He did, his eyes lighting up and his face taking on

an expression of exaggerated ecstasy that made me laugh. "This," he said, holding the remains of cookie number one aloft, "is beyond a doubt the best cookie I ever ate in my life."

Something wonderful happened to me at that moment.

I fell in love.

And I sure hoped this guy never met Joanie.

JOHNNY ATE SO MANY cookies at that Fourth of July celebration I was afraid he'd get sick. He also insisted on paying for all but the first two. At a quarter for two cookies, he contributed greatly to club coffers.

All the girls gave him the eye and whispered about "the new boy." When they realized I "knew" him, they swarmed around me and I let them drag out what particulars I had, which wasn't all that much. Even Joanie sauntered up, her expression mischievous.

"What are you doing, Frankie? Trying to cut my time?"

I know I blushed. "Don't be silly. There's no chance of that."

"Umm. .I'm beginning to wonder." She laughed out loud. "Don't look so shook up. You see your chance, you grab it! There are enough boys to go around, even cute ones." With a conspiratorial wink, she wandered away.

At about four-thirty, Johnny approached our booth yet again. The celebration was beginning to wind down with many people heading for the parking lot. Most would return later for the fireworks display that would start after dark.

"No more cookies!" I cried in mock horror, pretending his arrival didn't mean a thing to me. "I don't want you to overdose."

He smiled the smile that melted my heart. "Aren't you about ready to finish up here?" he inquired.

"Getting close. Carrie's counting the money—" I indicated my friend at the end of the counter "—and that will be it."

"Great. I was thinking…" He looked a little bashful as he spoke. "Maybe you could show me the town. We only got here a couple of days ago, and I've been too busy to look around."

"I don't think my mother would ever let me go out with a strange boy."

"Already asked her," he said a bit smugly. "She says okay, but to get you home by six."

"Wow, you work fast. I'm impressed." I hesitated. I wanted to go with him more than anything in the world, but at the same time, I was afraid. Not of him but of me. I'd never felt this way about any boy, even the one who gave me my first kiss.

Kiss. I shouldn't have thought about that. I knew beyond a doubt that Johnny's kiss would be entirely different from any I'd ever had, and I wasn't sure I was ready for it. Not that I thought he'd want to kiss me or anything, I thought hastily.

"You were saying…?"

I leaped into the breach, as my English teacher would say. "Sure. Okay, why not? Just a ride around town." I turned to Carrie, who wasn't in Future Home-makers, but had been conned into counting the money in the tin box. Being the smartest girl in school, she could be trusted to add everything properly.

"I'm checking out," I said. "Be sure the cash box

gets to Miss Pringle." Old Maid Pringle was our home ec teacher. "I'll be back tomorrow to help with clean-up."

"Hey, wait a minute!" Carrie said. "I'm not even a future homemaker—"

"Just this once, please?" My eyes pleaded with her.

Carrie took one look at me and just grinned. "Yeah, okay."

She was under no obligation but I had been sure she'd help me out. "Thanks! See you tomorrow."

And with that, I lifted the barrier between the safety of the booth and the uncertainty of a ride with this boy I'd just met.

NOBODY COULD BE as fascinated by our little town as Johnny seemed to be. He questioned everything, wanted the name of every business, remarked on the bygone "charm" of the place.

He made me laugh with every comment. He also made me wish I'd paid more mind to my grandpa's stories.

"Look, a building with a false front." He pointed, seeming impressed. "That's *really* old-fashioned."

"It is? I never paid any attention."

"Were there ever bank robbers or bandits around here?" He guided his red convertible to the curb, the engine idling.

"Bandits." I dredged up memories of tales told. "Well, they say that Jesse James came around a time or two. But then, I think every town in Missouri makes that claim."

He looked impressed so I added, "There was also a gunfight here way back when, but I don't know any details."

"Too bad. What got this town started? In the beginning, I mean."

"Mining." At last, something I knew. "Silicate and lead, mostly. There was actually a military skirmish east of here during the war between the states. Both North and South wanted our lead to make bullets."

"Wow." He pulled away from the curb, into a street with no other vehicles in sight. Still at the celebration, probably.

He brushed a hand over his forehead. "I don't know about you but I'm really getting warm. Is there anyplace open where we can get something cold to drink?"

"I've got the key to Reva's. We can go there. Mother won't mind."

"Great. Let's get a soda and find a place in the shade to drink it."

Sounded like a winner to me.

I SAT IN THE SHADE of a big old oak tree, my full skirt spread around me on the grass, and watched Johnny hard at work on carving something into the trunk with his pocketknife. I felt lazy and relaxed despite the oppressive heat and humidity, which beaded my face with moisture.

There's nothing like those steaming, muggy Missouri days to bring life to a standstill. I felt suspended in time, the only sounds the humming of insects and an occasional rustle of some creature in the overgrown grasses. Across a faraway barbed-wire fence, cattle grazed peacefully.

Johnny looked over with a quick grin. "I'll be through in a minute," he said. "Then you can see my masterpiece."

I nodded, somewhere in my own serene universe. Boys usually made me nervous, unless they treated me like a sister, but Johnny was different. In fact, we'd talked all the way during our drive around town.

We knew each other a lot better now, and I'd told him things I'd never mentioned to anyone else. I even told him that I didn't intend to go to college no matter who leaned on me to do so. That was about as big a secret as I had.

I intended to stay home, right here in this little town, and help Mother run Reva's. Someday it would be mine, and I would carry on in her tradition of good hometown food served to lots of nice people.

Johnny's plans were different. He planned to go to the University of California in Berkeley, his father's alma mater. He didn't seem so much excited as resigned.

Leaning back on braced arms, I lifted my face toward the sky. Dappled light made me close my eyes and I sighed with satisfaction. I'd forgotten to put on my new tanning solution—baby oil with iodine added. Joanie swore it would make my skin a glorious golden color.

After our tour and our stop by Reva's for bottles of pop, we'd ended up in this little unofficial roadside park just outside town. Happily we had it all to ourselves.

"Damn, that's good!"

I opened my eyes in time to see Johnny step back from the tree. He folded his pocketknife and slipped it into his jeans pocket. His white T-shirt was dark with perspiration. Crossing to me, he held out a hand.

I took it and he pulled me to my feet, then led me to

his side of the tree before releasing me. There, on the trunk inside a freshly carved heart, were the letters *FH + JD*.

I started to laugh. "Oh, Johnny, what are you thinking? We just met!"

He grinned down at me. "But I like you," he declared. "I just got this funny feeling when I met you. You're special. *We're* special. Don't you feel it?"

"I feel it." I touched the raw wood with a fingertip. "Nobody ever carved my initials before."

"The guys around here must be slow on the uptake." He caught me by the elbows and swung me around in front of him. "I don't know what it means, Frankie, but we just clicked—at least, for me we did. If I kiss you, will you scream?"

"There's nobody around to hear me except that old Jersey cow over there, and she won't care."

"In that case…" He slid his arms around my waist and exerted gentle pressure.

A car horn blasted the sultry air and I jumped back with a guilty start, my idyll broken. I could barely believe I'd been about to kiss a guy I just met.

A blue 1949 Ford with one green fender whizzed past, stirring up dust on the rocky dirt road. A burly arm waved out a window at us.

"Who's that?" Johnny asked, sounding annoyed.

"Jimmy, one of my brothers." The rat. Was that Joanie with him? Surely not. He already had a girl-friend, so he shouldn't be playing around.

At that precise moment of condemnation, panic struck. Maybe Jimmy was sending me a message. I gasped. "Omigosh, what time is it?"

So much for kisses. Johnny glanced at his big gold

wristwatch. "Six-thirty. Jeez! I've got to get you home!"

Hand in hand, we ran for the car. Instead of opening the door, he picked me up and swung me over the top, dropping me into the passenger seat. Then he piled in and thrust the key into the ignition. Not bad having a father who owned a bunch of Ford dealerships in Chicago. I'd never been in a convertible before this one and couldn't resist stroking the soft white leather interior.

The car started with a roar and Johnny steered it toward the road. The entrance was nothing more than a low spot across the ditch, down the way a piece. Johnny, apparently trying to save time, steered straight for the road, powering through low-growing greenery and bouncing over ruts and rocks.

I hung on to the door for dear life, hoping he knew what he was doing. And finding out the hard way that he didn't. The car suddenly jerked to a halt with the sound of screeching metal. To my horror, the front end began to rise slowly from solid earth.

I screamed and Johnny cussed, then cut it short and gave me a stricken look.

"I've heard the language," I yelled at him. "I've got three brothers! Just tell me what happened!"

"I don't know. I gotta look."

He jumped out of the car and worked his way through tall, prickly brush to the front end, where he began to mutter words I fortunately couldn't make out. When he returned, though, he looked cheerful enough.

"We've run up on a downed fence post," he explained. "It got hooked on something underneath. Don't worry, we'll be loose in a jiffy."

A jiffy seemed a trifle optimistic to me, but I let his confidence sweep me along.

WE DROVE UP TO my house a little after eight. It wasn't fully dark yet but the sky was heading in that direction. Once we finally freed the car, I'd been overwhelmed by dread.

"My dad's going to kill me," I said for the tenth time as Johnny pulled the car to the curb. It wasn't running too well now, the front tires wobbling instead of going straight. Even I knew enough about cars to figure the alignment was seriously out of whack.

"Frankie, I'm sorry. I can't tell you how sorry."

"It's not your fault." I jumped out of the car. "I was the one who should have been paying attention to the time."

"It's my fault, so don't argue." He got out of the car and slammed the door, then walked around to my side. "Come on," he instructed, holding out his hand.

"What are you doing?"

"I'm going with you so I can tell your father what happened, and that I'm to blame."

"Please—you don't know my dad. Don't, Johnny!"

"I have to," he said flatly, his expression grim. "We'll face the music together."

Hand in hand, we walked up the curved driveway. I didn't know about him but my heart was in my throat.

CHAPTER THREE

MY FATHER LOOMED in the doorway, his face a thunder-cloud. Johnny's hand tightened on my hand and then he released it and stepped forward resolutely.

"Sir, it's my fault," he said in a voice so firm yet at the same time full of repentance. "I ran into a little problem with the car—"

"You wrecked your car with my daughter in it?" my father bellowed. "You idiot—"

My mother appeared behind him. "Now, Mike, give him a chance to explain."

My father sneered at us. "You heard her," he snapped. "Explain."

So Johnny did. He told the honest truth and I never opened my mouth, totally impressed with his straight-forward manner and apparent lack of fear. My father listened, his face stern and unforgiving.

"And that's how it happened," Johnny concluded. "I hope you won't forbid me from seeing Frankie, but if you do, please don't punish her because this wasn't her fault."

My heart skipped a beat and I gave him a distress-ful glance. Not see each other anymore? I'd never be able to stand that.

For the longest time, my father glared at us beneath

the flickering illumination of the porch light, surrounded as it was by a mass of circling insects. Finally
he seemed to make up his mind.

His expression lightened and he let out a grunt. "I'll
give you one thing, boy, you've got gumption."

"Thank you, sir."

"It wasn't a compliment."

"Then I apologize, sir."

"It took a lot of guts for you to bring Frankie to the
door after missing her curfew the way you did. Most kids
your age would have dropped her at the sidewalk and
run."

"Daddy!"

"I doubt that," Johnny said staunchly. "Frankie isn't
the kind of girl a guy would 'drop off.' I have great
respect for her."

"In that case," my father said, "I won't ground her or
sic your folks on you or send her brothers out looking for
you. You've acted like a man and I respect you for that."

"Thank you, sir." Johnny stood tall. "It will never
happen again."

"Damn right, it won't. It does and you'll be so far up
that famous creek nobody will ever hear your name
again."

I threw my arms around my father in gratitude. I'd
expected untold miseries, but Johnny had handled
everything just right.

Which only proved what I'd expected from the
beginning: Johnny Davis was, quite simply, perfect.

JOHNNY WENT HOME and Mother went to fold laundry.
That left me alone with Daddy. Eager to get to my
bedroom where I could dream about my day, I was

waylaid when he pointed me into the living room. I perched on the edge of the sofa, my hands clenched in my lap, uncertain about what was coming. Off to one side of the room, the television set had some cowboy movie on the screen.

Daddy cleared his throat. "Frankie," he said, "there are a few things we need to get straight."

"Yes, Daddy," I said, completely in the dark.

He halted his pacing in front of me. "You're a good girl but you're naive. Boys will take advantage of you if you're not careful."

"Daddy Johnny would never—"

"I'm not just talking about Johnny. I'm talking about *boys*. All of 'em, every damned one. They're all alike when it comes to girls."

My cheeks burned with embarrassment. I *was* naive, no getting around it, but I wasn't stupid. Was this a birds-and-bees lecture? "Mom already told me this stuff," I managed to respond.

"Your mom was never a boy on the prowl," he snapped. "I was."

"You?" I stared at him, eyes widening. I'd never thought of my father as a boy. I'd certainly never thought of him being on the prowl.

"Don't get funny when I'm trying to make a point." He sounded put off by my astonishment. "I'm telling you to be suspicious of every boy who comes sniffing around because there's only one thing on his mind. I don't want my daughter to be led astray by some smart-ass kid who feeds her a line."

"Johnny didn't—"

"Forget Johnny. He's one of many, girl, and no different from the rest of them. You got that?"

"Yes, but—"

"No buts. As long as I can trust you, we'll do fine. It's up to the girl to draw the line because boys don't even know there *is* a line. They're out for what they can get, and they're not going to get it from my daughter."

I swallowed hard and said, "No, Daddy."

"I suppose now you're going to start wanting to go out on dates all the time. When you do, I don't intend to worry about what you're doing."

"I've been on dates before," I reminded him defensively. "Twice. You don't have to worry about me."

"Men always worry about their daughters, and you're the only one I've got." He ran a hand through his thinning hair. "You, I trust. Unfortunately, too many kids today are out of control. It's them I worry about, getting you into trouble. They've got no morals—listen to their music if you don't believe me. That Elvis-the-Pelvis guy should be thrown in jail for corrupting the younger generation."

I could have told him it was *my* music, too, and that Elvis made me and all my friends drool. If I did, though, I'd probably be locked up for the rest of the summer, so I just nodded.

"Honey…" His tone softened. "It's my duty to watch out for you. You have no idea how hard life can be for a girl who loses her reputation, if you know what I mean."

I knew what he meant. A girl in my class last year got pregnant and she had to drop out and move away in her shame. I thought at the time the boy who did it should be horsewhipped, but basically he got off scot-free.

I nodded again, my head down.

"Well, good," he said heartily and, I thought, with relief. "You're my pride and joy, Frankie. You're too good to get messed up with any of these local yokels. Live a good, clean life and hold your head high until the right man comes along."

"Yes, Daddy." I rose and gave him a quick, kind-of-nervous hug. I was absolutely certain that I'd never get into the kind of trouble he referred to. "I'll make you proud, Daddy. You don't need to worry. You and Mom set a great example and I'll always follow it."

"Yeah, well—" He stepped back as if shy. "Run along now and see if your mother needs any help. I've gotta give Jeff a hand with his car. Thinks he's this great mechanic but he don't know anything about that Packard."

As it turned out, Daddy should have given that lecture to Jeff and to heck with the car.

MY SIXTEENTH SUMMER settled into the happiest time I could remember. I helped out at Mom's diner, which I loved, and I went out with Johnny when I wasn't working. I'd never had a steady boyfriend before. In fact, before Johnny came to town, I'd had only a couple of forgettable dates. I was absolutely crazy about Johnny, but cautious, too. I didn't intend to break my promise to my father…if I could possibly help it.

Then everything busted loose at home. Johnny had taken me to see a movie that night. Since it was dark when we got home, I risked a quick kiss before I hopped out of the car. Johnny whispered, "Tomorrow?"

"Yes," I replied happily.

Running up the driveway, I realized there was an extra car here, a Buick I didn't recognize. Maybe my folks had a new couple over to play cards, which was about their only recreation.

The door stood open, and as I reached for the screen I heard Daddy's voice.

"Just a damned minute! Are you telling me that this girl is—"

"Her name is Debbie, not 'this girl'!" Jeff yelled. I'd never heard him speak to our father that way.

Opening the screen door, I eased inside and turned right, hesitating in the large open doorway to the living room. Standing there were Daddy and Jeff, Mother, Jeff's girlfriend, Debbie, and her parents, Mr. and Mrs. Rivers, who owned the filling station.

Nobody even noticed me, which suited me fine. I wanted to know what was going on, of course, but I had a sinking feeling that I knew.

Mrs. Rivers said in a wobbly voice, "Mike, this isn't getting us anywhere. What's done is done. Now we have to decide what—"

"The hell we do! Jeff's too young to be getting married. Hell, he doesn't even have a decent job. Your girl should have had better sense than to—"

Jeff yelled, "I'm twenty-one and I work at the bowling alley and play with a band! I don't need your permission." Almost as an afterthought, he added, "And it wasn't all Debbie's fault, either, so don't give her a hard time."

Tears streamed down Debbie's cheeks and she looked even younger than her nineteen years. "Why did we even come here, Jeff? I don't want to get married." She turned to Mrs. Rivers. "I told you that, Mother. I don't want a baby. I'm going to get rid of it!"

That last comment struck everyone silent and we all

stared at her as if she'd lost her mind. Was she talking about giving up the baby or something worse? Abortions were illegal. Sometimes the operation killed the mothers as well as their babies, or so I'd heard.

"Over my dead body!" Mrs. Rivers gave her daughter such a shake. "You will marry this boy and have his baby and—"

"*His* baby?" Daddy raised his voice and a heavy eyebrow. "How do we know it's his baby?"

"Mike Hale!" Mother spoke, her eyes flashing. "Debbie is a good girl."

"Good girls don't get pregnant out of wedlock."

"That's not always true and you know it!" She stood right up to him, her shoulders square and her jaw thrust out. "I think you better get off that train of thought *right now*."

Daddy glared right back at her. "You want the boy to get married?"

"Yes! It's the right thing to do. If he didn't want to marry, he shouldn't have done what he did."

"Aw, Mom." Jeff scuffled his feet, his face miserably downcast. "We were just fooling around and things got out of hand. Do I have to?"

Debbie gave him a shove. "I said I don't want to get married! Not to you and not to anybody. I want to move to Kansas City and get a job and have fun for once."

"You can't do that while you're pregnant, Debbie," Mrs. Rivers commented weakly.

The girl burst into tears again. "Why is this happening to me?" she wailed. "If I get married, my life is over!"

I knew why it was happening to her. She didn't

think about the consequences of her actions. She didn't get good advice from her parents, like I did. Or if she did, she didn't pay attention. I wasn't like Debbie. I'd never be like her, although every time Johnny touched me I felt as if I'd die.

He would probably be easier to resist as time went by. His magic would fade or I'd grow stronger or…something, because I had my pride. I'd never end up like Debbie.

Mom looked around the circle of people. "I think it's time for you men to go find something else to do," she said. "Ada and I will talk to Debbie, and you, Jeff, you're not going anywhere." She steered Debbie onto the sofa and pointed to Jeff and then to the seat beside the trembling girl.

Daddy said, "Now, Mary—"

Mom said "Git!" and pointed to the doorway, spotting me standing there for the first time. Her eyes narrowed slightly but she didn't order me away, to my surprise. Maybe she thought this would teach me a good lesson.

Mr. Rivers got up and followed Daddy out. The mousy little man had not said a single word and seemed grateful to leave.

I glanced at Mom. "I'll go make coffee," I said.

"Good idea. We're going to need it. Now getting back to you two kids—"

I DIDN'T WANT TO tell Johnny what had happened that day. At first, I just couldn't. I wasn't sure how he'd react, or how I'd react when he did. Jeff had done something wrong but he was my brother and I loved him.

I thought about Jeff and Debbie a lot. It didn't seem

fair to force them into marriage, but what would happen to her if she struck out on her own? What if she had the abortion and it killed her or something? There'd be enough guilt from *that* to go around. If she gave away the baby, could she live with herself? Would she look at every baby she saw and long for her own?

But if she and Jeff actually tried to make a go of a new little family, would either of them be happy? I wondered but I didn't say a word to Johnny. Until he gave me a quizzical look and asked the dreaded question.

"What's all this gossip about your brother and that Rivers girl?"

I hesitated. I couldn't lie to him. Not only was I a rotten liar—people always saw through me—but lying was dishonorable and my conscience would hurt me something awful.

I sighed. "I hoped you wouldn't ask me about that."

"Why not?"

"Because it's sort of…not good." He didn't say anything, just looked at me expectantly. "Jeff got his girlfriend pregnant and now they have to get married."

"*Have* to?" He didn't look convinced.

"That's what Debbie's mom and my mom say. Jeff has to live up to his responsibilities."

"How about the girl?"

"Debbie doesn't really want to get married to *anyone,* and neither does Jeff. She wants to go to Kansas City and have fun, and he wants to play in a big-time band."

He looked sympathetic to their plight. "It'll be tough on both of them with a baby."

"She doesn't want the baby, and Jeff sure isn't in any

position to handle it. I feel awful telling you that but she's even mentioned…abortion." I whispered the last word. "Her mother went crazy when she said it."

Johnny shook his head slowly. "So they're getting married anyway?"

"They don't have much choice."

"There's always a choice," he said. "Always. I hope it works out for them."

"So do I."

And for us, I thought, sensing dangerous days ahead.

THE JEFFERY HALE-Deborah Rivers wedding was set for 2:00 p.m., twenty-seven days following that big confrontation. As Debbie's maid of honor, I waited upstairs with her for the Big Entrance, trying to be helpful but wishing I was anywhere else.

Debbie had the prettiest bedroom I'd ever seen. Everything was pink and white and lacy. She even had a makeup table with a lighted mirror and a multitude of cosmetics.

Against the back wall, French doors opened onto her very own balcony, furnished with a small round metal table and two matching chairs. Two flowerpots hooked to the balcony rail spilled trails of white flowers over the sides and down to the deck floor.

This room, I thought, *is fit for a movie star, and she'd be leaving it all after the wedding.* No wonder she didn't want to marry Jeff!

The bride herself slumped on the chair before the makeup table. She wore a beautiful white dress, and a veil perched on top of her blond hair. Her face as pale as the dress, she seemed composed if not happy.

I gave her a careful hug, not wanting to mess up

anything. "It will be okay," I whispered into her ear. "Jeff's a nice guy, mostly. Once you have the baby—"

"I'm giving it away," she said flatly. "I don't want a baby. If my folks won't take it, I'll find somebody who will. They can make me get married, but they can't make me be a mother when I don't want to be."

Shocked, I stared at her grim face. "But what about Jeff? Does he think this is a good idea?"

She gave a bitter little laugh. "Jeff doesn't think, period. All he wants is to play with a rock 'n' roll band and become rich and famous. He doesn't care a lick what I do with the baby."

I doubted that, I really did. Jeff was no great thinker, but we'd been raised to believe that all married couples wanted kids.

"What do you want to do that's more important than raising your own flesh and blood?"

She gave me a fierce look. "Don't you get snippy with me, little girl. You don't understand anything."

I understood that she was in a heck of a mess and half the responsibility was hers. I didn't say that, though, knowing it wasn't a good idea to upset the bride any more than I already had.

"I'm sorry," I said, as humbly as I could. "I don't want to make things worse, and it's none of my business."

Debbie drew a deep sigh, reaching out to pat my hand. "You're a good girl, Frankie. Let this be a terrible lesson to you. I knew what Jeff wanted and like a fool, I gave it to him."

"If you knew, then why—"

"You *are* young." She looked at me in disbelief. "I

wanted it, too. He got me all worked up and you know what happened." She shrugged. "Not as if it was a surprise. Jeff wasn't my first and he knew it, but I sure don't want my mother to know *that*. I'd never been caught, so I thought I could get away with it forever, I guess."

"You messed around with other boys?" I frowned. "Then how do you know it's Jeff's baby?"

"I only had one boyfriend at a time," she exclaimed indignantly. "What do you think I am, a slut?"

She looked so pissed off that I wasn't about to tell her that yes, I did think she was a slut. How stupid was I not to even imagine that girls would sleep around like that? "I'm sorry," I said to placate her. "I didn't mean—"

"It's okay," she interrupted. "You're just a kid. You'll wise up. We all do."

"I wish I could do something to help you," I said hesitantly. "I know—I'll babysit for you."

"I told you, I'm not keeping the baby." She looked completely exasperated now. "Maybe I'll get lucky and fall down the stairs and put an end to this whole thing." She shifted awkwardly in the chair, clenching her hands over her belly.

"Oh, don't say that." Not that I'm superstitious but saying such things invites trouble. Watching her, I frowned at her restlessness "Are you all right? You don't look comfortable."

"I'm okay, or as okay as I can be. Frankie, go peek and see if they're about ready to start this thing. I'm fed up with waiting. I guess being married will be better than having my mother for a bodyguard for the rest of my life, which is what she's been ever since she found out."

"Okay." I hesitated, feeling uneasy. "I'll be right back."

"Take your time."

To my regret, I did.

CHAPTER FOUR

I PEERED OVER THE banister so I could look at the scene below in the small entryway of the Rivers house. To the left, I could see just a sliver of the room where the wedding would take place. It looked as if the few chairs were filled and everything was ready to begin. Johnny sat in the last row, looking wonderful in a suit and tie. He glanced up, smiled, nodded.

Few people had been invited, due to the circumstances, not that any of this would remain secret.

My mother appeared in the entryway, dressed in a pretty blue mother-of-the-groom dress. She wasn't smiling, and motioned me to come down and join her.

I scurried down the stairs, holding up my floaty pink gown. I know girls in weddings always hate what they have to wear, but not me. This was by far the nicest dress I'd ever owned, thanks to Mother's skill with the sewing machine.

"How's Debbie doing?" she asked.

"Not great," I said, adding hopefully, "She's not hysterical, though." I chewed on my bottom lip, remembered I was wearing Revlon Fire and Ice lipstick and stopped. "Mom, is this really a good idea?"

She didn't pretend not to understand. "I don't know," she said. "Probably not, but the thought of an illegitimate baby was more than Ada could handle—and I'm not too crazy about it, either. Debbie's an only child and this has about destroyed her mother. Speaking of whom..."

Mom looked past my shoulder and I turned to see Mrs. Rivers scurrying toward us. Her dress was champagne lace.

"It's time," she said, the deep lines around her mouth revealing her tension. "Frankie, dear, will you tell Debbie it's time to start the ceremony?"

"Yes, Mrs. Rivers."

I turned toward the stairs but could hear Mother's words. "Now, Ada, don't fall apart on me. Just a few more minutes and they'll be safely married. Then we can work on them about the baby."

I thought I heard a muffled sob, but I didn't turn around.

When I reached Debbie's room, she wasn't there. She must be in the bathroom, I deduced. I knocked lightly on the door, pressing my cheek close so I could hear. "Debbie? It's time."

No response.

"Debbie? They're waiting for us." I knocked a little harder, and the door swung open. On the tiled bathroom floor lay a white wedding gown and no sign of Debbie.

My heart stopped beating and my stomach clenched into a knot. This couldn't be happening. She wouldn't just take off minutes before her wedding, would she? Jeff would be humiliated. Maybe not, but our mother and Debbie's certainly would be.

Trembling with anxiety, I hurried back into the bedroom and looked around wildly, then dashed across to the French doors. One stood slightly ajar. I flung it wide and rushed onto the balcony.

"Debbie!" I couldn't scream under the circumstances. Leaning against the railing, I bent over to look down. Not a sign of her amongst the masses of lilac bushes fighting for space. How would she get down from here?

She probably had a getaway route developed over years of sneaking out to meet boys. Time to face the music, Frankie. You get the joy of telling the world that we've got a runaway bride.

My skirt swishing around me, I hustled down those stairs and up to my mother.

She looked up at the landing and asked, "Where is she?"

"She's gone," I whispered.

"What? Gone where?"

"I don't know where. While I was down here talking to you, she ducked out the back way, I guess."

"You guess?"

"Well, she's not there!"

"Oh, my God. Go get Jeff. Where's Ada? I've got to tell Ada." She scanned the room, trying to spot Mrs. Rivers.

Jeff stood at the makeshift altar at the front of the living room, shifting from one foot to the other and looking as if he expected a firing squad to appear at any moment. Next to him stood Jimmy, the best man. I had to admit they both looked darned good in their rented tuxes and ruffled shirts, if you didn't notice their expressions.

Jeff looked terrified; Jimmy looked bored silly. I hurried to the bridegroom's side and whispered into his ear.

"Mom wants you."

"What for?"

I decided to put him out of his misery. "Debbie's disappeared."

"What are you talking about?" He said it with a wild light of hope in his eyes.

"Debbie ran out the back. I have no idea where she's gone."

He looked toward heaven and breathed a soft, "Thank you, Lord!" before loping to the front of the room for a whispered conference with Mom. Ada joined them, looking panicky before she even got there. Once she heard the news she let out a shriek and collapsed on the floor in a heap.

That pretty much did it. Guests erupted from their seats and surrounded the threesome in the entryway, everyone talking at once. Daddy bulled his way through, his voice penetrating. "I *told* you women this was a bad idea, but you had to have your way."

I stood there looking at the chaos, sorry I'd invited Johnny to this debacle. Somehow I'd known things wouldn't go smoothly today.

I looked down at my candy-pink dress, wondering if we'd reached the point where I might as well change clothes. There wouldn't be any wedding here today. Even if they caught Debbie, I doubted anybody could make her say "I do" when she obviously didn't. I saw no point in staying to watch that coming train wreck.

On the other hand, I was supposed to be the maid of honor and I probably should feel a lot worse than I did. How selfish could I be? Poor Debbie was out there alone running heaven knew where, her mother had been humiliated, my mother right there with her, and my rotten brother was ready to throw a party.

Maybe I should go looking for the bride while everyone else headed for the front door. It was probably my fault she ran away since I left her alone when I shouldn't have.

Johnny appeared and slid an arm around my waist. "Whoa!" he said. "This is the wildest wedding I ever went to."

"How many would that be?"

"Counting today?" He considered. "One."

That made me smile. "I'm glad you're here, too, I guess," I said. "I wouldn't want to have to explain all this and try to get anyone to believe it."

"I don't know," he said, teasing me. "Runaway bride, groom left at the altar… I've heard of stuff like this. I don't know if you noticed, but your brother didn't exactly look brokenhearted when he got the—"

A deep, masculine voice interrupted him, hollering out the news. "We found her! It was a horrible accident—she fell off the roof. Her daddy's taking her to the hospital now."

Accident? I wondered. Falling off the roof was less suspicious than throwing yourself down the stairs in front of witnesses.

I WENT TO SEE Debbie the day before she was to be released from the hospital. I didn't really want to, but Mom said I should, even though the wedding would never be. Debbie got her wish and had lost the baby, so there was no reason to beat that dead horse.

I entered her room with gifts—a bouquet of flowers

and a box of chocolates. "Mmm," Debbie said. "My favorite."

She took the box of candy from my hand and ripped it open. I turned, looking for something to put the flowers in. Seeing nothing, I laid them on the bedside table.

Debbie looked healthy to me, all propped up on pillows and wearing her own pretty blue nightgown, not one of those ugly hospital things. Her color was good and her eyes sparkled. I doubt anything could have made her happier than the chocolates she lifted to her mouth.

Swallowing, she licked her lips. "I'm sorry I had to sneak out on you that way, honey," she said, reaching out to squeeze my hand and leaving chocolate smears on my knuckles. "At the last minute, I just couldn't go through with it."

"You mean, go through with falling down the stairs?" I felt mean saying that, but what she'd done wasn't any too nice, either. Her actions had turned the wedding into a circus and had hurt a lot of people, the groom excluded.

She looked at me with suddenly cool blue eyes, her lips curving in a half smile. "You think I fell off the roof on purpose?"

"Did you?"

She considered for a moment. "I don't think I'll answer that," she said at last. "I'll just let you worry about it. My guess is that you haven't told anyone what I said to you, about the stairs, I mean."

"No."

"That's good. If they knew about that crack I made, they'd probably lock me up somewhere. Besides, my mom's upset enough already."

"My mom, too. She's so mad she kicked Jeff out of the house."

"I'm sorry to hear that, when he was all prepared to 'do the right thing.'"

"Mom will let him come back home once she cools down, but what about you, Debbie? What are you going to do now that there's no baby and the wedding's off?"

Her lips curved in a secretive little smile. "It's for sure I can't stay around here, with all the gossip—not that I'd want to stay around this hick town under any circumstances. I have a friend in Kansas City so I'm going there."

"Just like you hoped." Oh, my evil tongue! "Is this a girl friend or a guy friend?"

She laughed. "Wouldn't you like to know! Look, I appreciate you dropping by, but I'm expecting my mother anytime now. She's still upset, and I don't think you want to get in the middle of that."

"No, thanks." I turned toward the door and stopped with my hand on the knob. "Tell the truth, Deb, was it an accident?"

The look on her face told me all I needed to know.

Her laughter followed me into the hall.

SUMMER MOVED along quickly. Debbie relocated to Kansas City, over her mother's grieved disapproval. Mrs. Rivers and my mother had become fast friends since sharing that double blow from their children. Mom let Jeff move back home in early September, and school started for me the day after Labor Day.

What a difference it made to have a real boyfriend. We shared a couple of classes, ate lunch together, studied together, made out together every chance we got. My friends looked at me with envy because Johnny was so cute and had a cool car and was really nice on top of it. Could this be happening to me?

All of a sudden, I actually liked school. I'd always gotten good grades without too much effort, and I continued to do so, but I was torn. I wanted to graduate from high school with the rest of the class of 1964 but at the same time, I *didn't* want to graduate. Once I did, I'd lose Johnny—his dad wanted him to spend next summer in Chicago learning the car dealership business. Then he'd leave for California in the fall to study business. California sounded a million miles away. He'd forget me. I couldn't stand the thought.

I had no interest in going to college. I wanted to work in my mother's café and someday, when she got old, take it over. I loved to cook and I loved to serve, maybe not as much as I loved Johnny, but it was enough.

We went to homecoming together and I went to every single one of his baseball games and cheered him on. For Christmas he gave me a friendship ring, which Mother wouldn't let me wear. Instead, I carried it on a golden chain around my neck, vowing that someday it would be on my finger.

As it turned out, that time would never come because sometime during the school year, the chain broke and I lost my ring. Johnny readily forgave me, pointing out that it was just an accident.

"Someday I'll get you a ring that you can wear on your finger," he said. "One that will be much more important than a friendship ring."

Nevertheless my anxiety grew. All this would come to an abrupt end in the spring, which loomed over me like a black cloud. I became more nervous with every

passing day. By the time I walked across the stage at
Fairweather High School in my white cap and gown to
receive my diploma, I was close to collapsing. After the
ceremony, after the cake and punch and congratulations, most of the senior class grabbed their swimsuits
and took off for Showe Creek to picnic and swim and
celebrate.

Johnny and I went along, but my interest was nil. I
tried not to cling to him, but I could barely help it.
Wearing my new blue one-piece swimsuit, I let the icy
current sweep me against him. He held me there, something deep and questioning in his blue eyes.

"Have a beer!" Ron Baker threw the open glass
bottle through the air, foamy liquid spraying out in a
curved sweep. Johnny caught it deftly. Ron always
took up a collection and brought beer because his older
brother worked at the Grab and Gulp at the edge of
town.

"Want one, Frankie?"

"No, thanks." I'd tried it once, which I'm sure my
parents never suspected, but I just didn't like the taste
of beer. Johnny rarely drank, but this time he swigged
down the beer as if he were dying of thirst.

"Let's get out of here," he said, his voice low and tight.

That tone cut right through me, bringing a flush to
my cheeks. I knew what he was feeling; I knew what
I was feeling.

"Your beer—"

"Finished." He tossed the empty onto the bank. "I
want to be alone with you, Frankie."

"I…" I swallowed hard, knowing without knowing. Dreading but anticipating. "I want that, too. Oh,
Johnny—"

"Let's go."

Holding my hand, he pulled me through the water toward the bank, and I went willingly. It seemed I'd been waiting a long time for this, halfway wanting it, halfway fearing it I would have to be strong enough to pull back before it was too late, but would I even know when that moment came? I wasn't like Debbie. I knew right from wrong, but I knew nothing about what was coming.

ISOLATED FROM the world, we lay side by side on the grass beneath the shade of a grove of oak trees. I felt as if I'd slipped into some kind of trance, soothed by the warmth of the day and Johnny's hands moving with tingling ease across my skin above and below the swimsuit

"I don't want you to go away this summer," I whispered.

"I don't want to go, either, but I have to. Dad's been patient with me staying here since he and Mom split, but he's the one who pays the bills. I can't spit in his face."

"I know," I admitted miserably. "But Chicago and then California—Johnny, I think I'll die without you."

His hand slid beneath the top curve of my swimsuit, and I caught my breath, automatically lifting my breast into his hand.

"We'll always be together, Frankie. I've realized for a long time that we're meant for each other. Don't you know that I...I...love you?"

"You've never said that to me before."

"It's hard." He looked past me, into the trees. "It's the way I was brought up, Frankie. Nobody in my family shows much emotion about anything. It's different with you, though."

"I'm glad."

He looked down at me, his expression a little uncertain. "How do you feel now, honey? Am I going too fast for you?"

"What do you think?" I snuggled closer to him. I wanted to laugh with relief. "I've loved you from the day we met. But being separated for a whole year…it's scary. Things happen. You'll meet other girls…"

"You'll meet other guys, but who gives a damn? I trust you. Don't you trust me?"

"Yes, but— Oh!" His thigh pressing between mine cut off all reasonable thought. I'd never let anyone touch me like that before and now I wondered why. Why? Ripples of something I didn't understand coursed through my stomach and I felt my nipples tighten.

"Frankie." He buried his face in the hollow of my shoulder and neck, breathing hard. "You're so innocent. I don't want to do anything you're not ready for, but…jeez, I want you so bad."

"I w-want you, too, Johnny." My mother would kill me for this, but I didn't know if I could stop, especially since I really didn't want to. Not now when this could be our very last time together.

"Are you afraid?"

"A…a little bit."

"Don't be, baby. I won't hurt you, I promise. There…"

I groaned, barely able to stand these new and powerful sensations. I knew what could happen if I gave in to my feelings, but Debbie had said she'd been lucky for a long time. I could be lucky, too.

His lips came down hard on mine and after one last brave moment, I gave myself over and let him in.

CHAPTER FIVE

TWO WEEKS FOLLOWING graduation, Johnny and his mother headed for Chicago, leaving me abandoned in Fairweather. That's how I felt, but at least I had memories. Beautiful memories, along with a world of dread.

Never in my wildest dreams had I thought that I could be so wild about a boy that I'd forget everything my parents had ever taught or told me. I had been so very certain that I would be strong when this day came, but I was wrong. Johnny and I made love that first time in the heated atmosphere following graduation. In the cold light of day, I assured myself it would never happen again.

But it did, as naturally as flowers blossomed. That's how I felt, like a flower unfolding its petals to the sun. Just touching his hand made me want more and more of him. Each time he asked me if I was sure, I uttered a heartfelt "Yes!"

Now, at *last*, I understood what the fuss was all about. Sex wasn't something you could think about rationally. It grabbed you by the throat and wouldn't let go. Even knowing all the risks didn't deter me. A little bit was not enough; I always wanted more. At night I'd lie in my bed and wonder what in the world had happened to me.

And was glad, deep down, that it had.

Usually he had rubbers, but not always. They were hard for him to come by, especially since he wanted to protect my reputation by not going to anyone who knew us to snag a few.

But still, he left me. In his absence, I pined for him, to quote my mother, but I also kept busy. I worked at Reva's and palled around with my girlfriends, when they had time left over from their boyfriends, and went to movies and such.

Johnny called a few times, but I always got the feeling he was really busy. A time or two I even heard his father calling him in the background. He couldn't say anything important, like "I love you."

I was pleased when Joanie invited me to a sleepover. "Just a few of us," she explained. "You, me, Carrie and Brenda. Got any new records you can bring? I just got a new Bobby Darin I just love."

"Oh, I like Bobby, too. I'll bring my Beach Boys. Should I bring anything else?"

"Of course! Bring your curlers and we'll do one another's hair. I cut this article out of a magazine on how to put on makeup like the stars. We'll be gorgeous."

"Or something. How about I bring some potato chips and California dip?"

"Great. Mom got us some pop and I'm making brownies so we won't starve. Come at six."

"I'll be there."

I welcomed the distraction. Maybe the party would take my mind off you-know-who.

WE SAT AROUND on the floor in Joanie's bedroom, wearing our pj's, hair in rollers, cold cream on our faces and surrounded by stacks of 45s.

"Do you like the Supremes?" Joanie asked everyone. She helped herself to the box of tissues, then passed it on.

Carrie shrugged. "Not so much. Don't you have any jazz in that pile of wax? Maybe some Louis Armstrong?"

"I don't even know what jazz sounds like!"

We all laughed about that because the rest of us didn't, either. "Here's some Elvis," Joanie announced. "That should suit everybody."

Everyone except my father. I giggled and reached for one of the big rollers in my hair. "When can I get out of these things?"

"Don't whine," Brenda ordered. "Just remember, we must suffer to be beautiful."

Joanie agreed with a solemn nod. Carrie sneered and made a rude sound, dabbing at her face with a tissue. She didn't normally curl her hair, just let it fall down her back, but she played along with us this time.

She had the longest hair I'd ever seen and now it was coiled around the biggest rollers Joanie owned. Carrie said she was growing her hair out so she'd fit in when she rebelled against society, which she fully expected to do when she got around to it.

Now that I thought of it, Carrie had been weird even as a little kid, but she was smart, too. She turned those probing eyes toward me and said, "So what are you doing this summer now that your boyfriend's gone?"

I felt immediately defensive. "He isn't gone, not for good, anyway. He still lives here."

"But he's in Chicago for the summer. And isn't he going away to college in September?"

I nodded glumly.

"Four years is a long time to be apart."

"We won't be apart, actually," I objected. "Not all the time. We'll write, and he'll be back for holidays and vacation and stuff."

"How does his mother feel about—"

"Carrie!" Joanie came to the rescue. "What's wrong with you? You can't ask questions like that!"

"Why not? It's better to ask than to listen to gossip."

"What gossip?" I asked.

"Oh, you know, the usual stuff—that you two broke up, that Johnny's going to live with his father from now on, that he left town because you're pregnant, that—"

"Pregnant!" The three of us said the word in horrified unison.

"Where did you hear *that?*" Brenda added.

Carrie shrugged. "I don't remember. I don't really believe it, though. You're such a Goody Two-Shoes, Frankie. You'd never date a boy who didn't live up to your lofty ideals. You wouldn't even let Elvis get you in a mess like that."

"Well," Joanie said, "maybe Elvis." She pursed her lips and gave me a suspicious look. "*Are* you?"

"Am I what?"

"Pregnant, like Carrie said."

"*No!* Are you crazy?"

"Come on, Frankie. It's obvious you two have been…you know. Going all the way."

I sputtered a denial. "J-just because *you* do doesn't mean everyone—"

"I never did! Only to second base…maybe once to third, but that's all."

Carrie said, "I never even went to first. There's nobody

around here worthy of my attention. That Willard Gerlock tried to kiss me once and I smacked him upside the head."

That lightened the moment and we all laughed. Willard was a year behind us in school and several inches shorter and pounds lighter than Carrie.

Suddenly Brenda said, "I've never gone all the way, either, but I'm going to."

Talk about shocking news. We stared at her in astonishment.

"Why ever for?" Joanie asked.

"Because if I don't, Larry's going to find someone who will." Her face suddenly looked as haggard as an eighteen-year-old's could. "He's already making eyes at Beverly Olsen and you know what a tramp she is."

Brenda looked absolutely miserable but determined, too. Carrie took her hand and squeezed hard.

"Don't do it, Brenda. Wait for the right guy to come along."

"Larry's the right guy and I love him so much," Brenda whispered. "If I g-get pregnant, he'll marry me and we can be happy."

Joanie leaned forward and stared into Brenda's eyes. "It won't work if you trap him that way. If he loved you, do you think he'd be checking out another girl?"

Carrie jumped into the effort to bring Brenda to her senses. I just sort of sat there and semi-listened, feeling like a total liar. If I hadn't gone all the way with Johnny, would he have found a girl who would? If I got pregnant—God forbid!—would he be there for me, or would he be another Jeff, forced into something he didn't want? Of course, Jeff dodged that bullet but not by his own doing.

Johnny's family would not react as mine and Debbie's had. They'd probably get him out of town fast and I'd be left alone with my humiliation. To have the whole town talking about me—

"Frankie!"

I started in surprise. "I'm sorry? What—"

"You're not paying any attention. This is important. It will affect Brenda's entire life."

"I know, Carrie, but who am I to give advice when I don't even know what I'm doing myself?"

Joanie laughed. "You always know what you're doing, Frankie. Never fear, girls." She gave the other two a conspiratorial glance. "I know a way to find out all Frankie's secrets."

"You won't find out anything about me," I informed her. "I'm not going to sleep a wink tonight!" Amidst their laughter, I started yanking curlers out of my hair and tossing them around the room.

"Now will somebody *please* do something about my hair? I want to look just like Natalie Wood."

By the time they finished with me, I looked more like Marjorie Main.

JOHNNY CAME HOME for a week before going away to school in California. By then I was in a state of panic since I'd heard so little from him over the summer. I vowed to be aloof, to make him suffer for his lack of attention.

My coolness lasted about five minutes.

Afterward, he leaned over to give me another kiss and whispered, "I missed you, Frankie. I didn't know how you'd feel by the time I got back."

I couldn't help laughing. "I guess that's cleared up." I sat up on the picnic blanket, which had been our bed, and struggled to don what I'd taken off. In the lowering dusk, I could barely see his face.

He sat up beside me and raked a hand through his tousled hair. "I'm sick to death of sneaking around and constantly trying to find the privacy to do what we want to do." He gave me a quick, sparkling grin. "It'll be even better in a bed."

"Maybe, but there's no way I'd go to a motel with you." I shuddered. "I'd die of embarrassment if someone found out."

"I know." He pressed his hand to the small of my back. After a moment he said, "You know it's going to be hard while I'm at school."

My throat tightened, and I couldn't force out a word so I nodded.

"I'm not going to ask you for any promises," he said then, the words cutting through me. "It wouldn't be fair to you."

"Fair to *me?* How about fair to you?"

"I'm not worried about me," he said. "I know how much I care for you. Frankie, I promise I'll be faithful."

"Meaning you won't sleep with any other girls while you're gone?"

"Well, yeah, for a start."

"Will you go out on dates?"

"There may be times when I'll be…you know, maybe just hanging with friends. I figure there'll always be girls around, just like in high school. I don't really know what college will be like, though. Maybe I won't have time to socialize."

"You'll be surrounded by girls," I said, feeling sorry for myself. "You'll forget all about me."

"Never." He leaned forward and pressed a kiss

below my ear. "There's so much I want to say to you, but somehow this doesn't seem like the time or place, not until I've proved myself."

"In that case," I said, getting to my feet, "I guess I'll have to prove myself, too. Of course, I won't have the same temptations you will. Fairweather's hardly a hot spot for great guys."

"Are you jealous?" He sounded surprised and rose to stand beside me.

"Jealous? Absolutely not." Embarrassed, I added, "You will write, won't you?"

"Of course. And call, too, when I get a chance."

"Wonderful." This wasn't at all the conversation I wanted and it certainly wasn't the time to throw my arms around him and declare my undying love. Not sure what to say, I simply blurted, "Look, it's been great, but I've got to get home."

"Okay. Mom's expecting me, too."

He put his arm around my shoulder and hugged me to his side, apparently not noticing my stiffness. "You're one in a million, you know that? This will all work out in time. Trust me."

And so I did, as much as I could.

WE SAID OUR GOODBYES on a blistering hot and humid late-summer day. Standing beneath autumn color, I didn't cry, although I wanted to. My emotions were all in a tangle. This didn't feel right, although it wasn't exactly a surprise. I'd known for a long time this separation was coming.

He held me in his arms and kissed my forehead. "I'm coming back," he murmured. "Never doubt that, Frankie."

"I know. It's just…I guess I didn't believe the time would come when you'd have to actually go."

"Me, either. We have to be patient, honey. I keep reminding myself that we'll have the rest of our lives together."

I wanted that more than anything in the world. As he drove away in his new blue convertible into a new world, I stayed behind in the old—and it still didn't feel right.

"It's Johnny's, isn't it?"

I buried my face in my pillow and wept. My mother had found me in the bathroom, head hanging over the toilet. She knew what I had suspected but denied for almost a month. Disgrace flooded over me in waves.

Her hands on my shoulders, she turned me around with gentle persistence. I didn't want to look at her, I felt such shame.

"Sweetheart." She smoothed wet hair away from my cheeks and drew a shuddering breath. "I thought more of that boy. To get you pregnant and then take off like he did—"

"He doesn't know, Mama," I sobbed. "How could I tell him? I didn't know myself until he'd already gone."

"Why didn't you come to me, dear? That's what mothers are for."

"I couldn't. I knew how disappointed you'd be in me. After what Jeff did—"

"Forget Jeff. How long did you think you could hide it, Frankie?"

The disappointment in her tone crushed me. Had she expected this? Maybe all along she'd feared that I'd turn into "that kind of girl" and now I had. I blinked to clear my damp eyes, wondering how this had happened to me. We'd been so careful—well, most of the time.

"I wanted to tell you, but I was so scared," I confessed. "I didn't believe it could be true and then I started getting sick in the morning—"

"Which is why they call it morning sickness."

"I guess." I sniffed and used the corner of the sheet to wipe my streaming eyes.

She sighed, a deeply mournful sound. "Frankie, do you have any idea why mothers worry so much about this sort of thing happening?"

"Th-the shame?"

"There's that, but the main reason is the way it messes up a girl's life. You're so young, only eighteen. To be saddled with an illegitimate baby at this age is awful. Your reputation will be shot, and you'll never find a man who'll respect you and marry you and make a home with you."

"But Johnny—"

"He's as young as you are, baby. He still depends on his parents for his livelihood, just like you do. He can't take care of a wife and family."

"He loves me and I love him."

"Do you believe everything he says to you?"

"Yes! He's not like other boys. He wants us to be together. It just has to be later, when he's finished with college."

She groaned. "Francine Hale, at your age you don't know love from a fence post. First you grow up and *then* you fall in love—with a man, not a boy."

"I'm in love whether you like it or not!"

"I *don't* like it, but I do know how you feel. Don't you think I remember?" A wistful expression softened her features and for a moment, I thought she really did know. "I was young once myself."

I said frantically, "He'll *want* to marry me when he finds out, Mama."

"Frankie, Frankie, the time isn't right. Do you want him to drop out of school, be tied down by a baby and a wife before he's even twenty years old?"

"What else can I do?" I had to stop crying like some big baby but I couldn't seem to get hold of myself.

"There are things that can be done."

I stared at her, horrified. "I could never kill my baby, if that's what you mean."

She shook her head. "That's not what I mean at all. I'm thinking…you could go stay with Aunt Eileen in Tulsa. When the baby comes, you can give it up for adoption."

"Oh, no, I wouldn't give up my baby. How could you ask me to do such a thing?"

"Aunt Eileen did."

My mouth gaped open. My beautiful, intelligent, successful aunt Eileen gave up a baby?

Mother patted my hand. "Nobody knows but the two of us, and now you. Let it sink in and we'll talk again later."

"Don't tell Daddy what I've done! Please!"

"There's no need for him to know at the moment. Maybe never."

"And my brothers." I groaned at the thought.

"I'd have to send out the sheriff to track them all down at the same time to do that the way they run in and out of this house. Believe me, they don't even know what day it is."

She bent over me. "As for you, try to calm down.

I'll tell everyone you have a touch of flu and they'll leave you alone while you think over what I've said."

"Mom, I love you."

"And I love you, sugar."

She kissed my cheek and rose. For the first time in ages, I closed my eyes and sleep actually seemed possible.

Present

SO FAR the drive had been grueling. The ice storm hadn't let up and Frankie witnessed more accidents and cars in the ditch than ever before in her life. Logic told her she needed to get off the road, find a hotel room and wait out the storm. But when it came to Johnny, her emotions beat out logic every time.

And so here she was, making slow progress toward Johnny.

When she stopped for gasoline, Frankie called the hospital, desperate for news. Holding her breath, praying she wasn't too late, she waited for Johnny's nurse to pick up the phone.

"There's some improvement," the nurse said. "We're expecting him to wake up soon. The doctor has confirmed that he had a heart attack, by the way."

A heart attack. That covered a lot of territory. "How much damage—" And at that point Frankie's cell phone cut out.

CHAPTER SIX

I DIDN'T WANT TO GO to Tulsa and give away my baby—no, never! But I also didn't want to bring shame and embarrassment on my family or me, or ruin Johnny's life and my own.

Mom brought my dinner on a tray, although I wasn't really sick. She fluffed pillows behind my back and positioned the tray on my lap. Then she sat down in a chair beside me.

"I spoke to Aunt Eileen," she said.

I flinched. "You told her I—"

"Honey," she interrupted, "if there's one person you can trust, it's my sister."

"I know." I chewed on my lip. "But before I make up my mind, there's something I have to take care of first."

Mom's eyebrows rose. "And that is?"

"I've written to Johnny."

"Oh, honey, do you think that's a good idea?"

"He has a right to know what I'm about to do. If he comes back to stop me…"

I think Mom sensed the frantic hope in my heart. I knew she'd still argue with me, though. Her mouth opened to say the words, but then her expression softened.

"If that's what you want, honey, that's what we'll do. Is that the letter?"

My fingers curled around the envelope. "Yes." I took a deep breath. "I know I have to do this, but it's hard."

She nodded. "I'll mail it for you. In fact, I need to go to the post office anyway to get some stamps."

"I don't know. Maybe I should do it myself." I held the envelope to my chest, strangely reluctant to let it out of my grasp but loathe to mail it. How could I trust the U.S. Postal Service with my life?

"Here." I thrust the letter at her, weak with hope and despair. If he didn't answer, I'd have to do something that every bone in my body resisted.

But to imagine being a mother? I didn't even know how to be a good daughter. I looked at Mom, so secure and comfortable with her role as mother; as a wife, so experienced and calm. She must be right about this. What did I know? How could I even begin to comprehend what it took to be a mother?

Mom smoothed the letter between her fingers. "I hope you get whatever answer you want, honey— whatever's best for both of you kids. In the meantime, I want you to know that Aunt Eileen would love to have you with her for as long as you'd like to stay. She'll make everything easy for you. When it's time, your baby will have a wonderful home and no one will know what you've been through."

No one but me, I thought. I would know. *Please, Johnny, don't let us down.*

I CRIED ALL THE way to Tulsa.

"Now, now, honey. This, too, shall pass," Mom said, patting my hand anxiously.

"I know, but—but he didn't even answer my letter! I thought he was so wonderful and now this." I spread my hands wide in frustration and disappointment. "How could I be so wrong?"

"He's just a boy," Mom said. "He wasn't ready to face it."

"But he said he loved me. And I know I l-love him."

"Frankie, listen to me." Mom's stern tone announced that she meant business. "You're young and inexperienced. This boy has let you down, but you'll be wiser the next time. True love will come when you're grown up and ready for it, baby."

I remembered the way Johnny made me feel, the lightness and the electricity. I was more than ready to experience love. If that wasn't it—

Maybe she was right. That startling new possibility brought my frantic thoughts up short. Love couldn't possibly hurt this much. I *was* foolish. I would forget Johnny, and then I'd meet a boy…meet a *man* who would mean it when he said he loved me. And I would love him back and never ever again think of the boy who broke my heart.

But I would always think of the baby I was going to give away, and try to come to terms with an action for which I'd carry shame and guilt the rest of my life.

Nice little Frankie Hale, an unwed mother. Fresh tears streamed down my cheeks and I sat there feeling sorry for myself the rest of the trip.

AUNT EILEEN met us at the door to her apartment. She swept me into her arms and kissed my forehead, then spoke to mother.

"I'm glad she's here. I know I can help her."

Mother nodded. "She's better off with you, for the time being. Thank you for doing this, Eileen."

I stepped out of my aunt's embrace and looked at the two sisters. They favored each other quite a lot, although Eileen was a woman of the world compared to my country-time mother. Mother's hair glinted with red lights but Eileen's glowed auburn and curled into a pageboy cut just like that of my favorite movie star, June Allyson. Eileen's blouse felt like silk and I knew Mother didn't own anything like that.

Eileen turned to lead us into the apartment. "Aren't you coming in, Mary?"

Mother shifted uncomfortably. "I have to get back home. Mike wasn't too happy I was driving so far today."

"He doesn't know what's going on, does he?"

"No, and he won't if I can help it."

"Good. Just the three of us…"

The four of us, I thought. Johnny knows. He just doesn't care.

This *had* to be the right thing to do. As much as I hated it, it must be right.

Mother left, and Aunt Eileen led me into her kitchen, where she fussed preparing two tall glasses of lemonade while I looked around. Everything in the apartment seemed to mirror her perfectly—no chintz or overstuffed furniture here. Instead she'd made her home sleek and modern, like herself.

Out of the blue, she said, "Are you angry with your mother?"

"Of course not. Why would I be?"

She shrugged. "There's always the possibility that she pushed you into coming here to have your baby."

I sighed. "I wasn't pushed," I said. "At least not by her. I made the decision myself."

"That's a relief." She carried the glasses to the small dinette table and put one before me. "I get the feeling that you're a much stronger girl than your parents believe."

I gave a nervous little laugh. "Sometimes I wonder," I said. "All I know is that I got in this mess myself and I have to get myself out—with a little help from my favorite aunt."

"Your only aunt," she said with a smile. She toyed with a napkin. "I'm sorry Mary couldn't stay," she said. "I see so little of her."

"Daddy doesn't like her to be gone," I said casually.

She let out a gust of breath. "I've always wondered why she puts up with that man." She glanced up and added, "I don't mean to criticize your father, but we've never really gotten along. He considers equal rights for women a joke. Forget equal! *Any* rights for women."

"I don't think he's *that* bad."

"He's that bad and worse." She literally gritted her teeth in frustration. "But there are changes coming. Many of us are banding together and laying plans for action. With federal and state commissions on the status of women—" She stopped short and gave an abrupt laugh.

Reaching out, she patted my hand. "Frankie, you've got the most blank look I've ever seen. You've got problems of your own and you couldn't care less about the women's movement for equal rights. Am I right?"

I ducked my head sheepishly and nodded.

"Never mind," she said. "Someday this will mean something to you, and to all women."

"You're involved in some kind of…women's movement?"

"Right up to my eyebrows. Which is why I'm unmarried and probably always will be."

I had to laugh at that. "You're no old maid," I protested.

"Honey, I'm forty-two and I've been working for a law firm for fifteen years. Trust me, that's an old maid." She grinned. "Technically, at least."

It seemed impossible. I thought she looked…I wasn't good at ages, but I'd guess thirty. She dressed fashionably, wore makeup beautifully, and I'd never seen her with a hair out of place.

"Your daddy," she said, getting back to the point, "is a tyrant."

Strong word, even if she and Daddy had never been pals. He considered her a wild woman who flaunted herself and her worldly goods, a bad influence on all his family. It must have been difficult for Mother to talk him into letting me come here.

Eileen took her empty glass to the sink and rinsed it out. "Frankie," she said, "don't ever be one of them."

"One of who?" I carried my glass to her.

"One of those old-fashioned wives who wait on their husbands hand and foot and ask permission for every little thing. That's the dark ages. Be your own woman!"

Dutifully I said, "I will, Aunt Eileen." I really didn't mean it. I wanted to belong to Johnny, but that dream had turned to dust. I'd probably end up being just like Aunt Eileen.

An old maid…

DADDY DIDN'T KNOW why I wasn't home for Christmas, but Mama told him Aunt Eileen had gotten me a job and

I couldn't get away. To keep up the fiction, I faithfully wrote letters to the family, telling them about all the adventures I shared with my aunt and at my job at a restaurant.

Time crawled past. I got to the point where I would hardly leave the apartment because it seemed as if all anyone had to do was look at me and they'd know I was that dreaded social phenomenon, the Unwed Mother-to-be.

My baby entered the world after what everyone assured me was an easy delivery—if that was easy, spare me the difficult. They wouldn't let me see the baby, wouldn't tell me the sex or anything else. Depressed and disbelieving, I cried and begged and pestered until Aunt Eileen reluctantly informed me I'd had a seven-pound-one-ounce baby boy who'd gone immediately to his new family, a doctor and his wife from Wichita.

"They're good people," she assured me. "They can't have a child of their own for some medical reason, so they'll give their new baby all the love and support in the world."

Their baby. I wanted to die.

Which I didn't, of course. I thought I'd never get over my grief but one day in June, I woke up and realized the sun shone, the birds sang, and I wanted to go home.

Aunt Eileen drove me back to Missouri that weekend, and I fell into my mother's arms with relief and gratitude. She'd kept my secret, not even driving to Oklahoma for the birth. She'd wanted to come, but getting around Daddy would have been difficult to impossible. Now she held me and wept through smiles of welcome.

Alone in my old room, I looked around as if I'd never seen it before. The childish decorations looked out of place on the wall now: school certificates, a corkboard with scraps of paper and fabric and trim tacked to its surface, the old wilted rose corsage from the senior prom, pinned to my gown by—

I wouldn't think about Johnny anymore—I wouldn't! I picked up that dried-out corsage and crushed it in my hand, the pearl-headed pin drawing blood. Childish dreams, all of it. My high-school days were behind me. I was through with Johnny Davis. I'd never speak to him again as long as I lived.

NOT VERY MANY of the kids in my graduating class went on to college. Once I was back from Tulsa and working at Mom's café, I saw just about all of them.

"I really envy you, Frankie," Joanie sighed over a chocolate malt. "I wish *I* had an aunt who lived someplace interesting." She glanced around with disdain. "Anything's an improvement over Fairweather. Why you came back I'll never know."

I swiped the wet dishrag across the counter. If she only knew. "This is home," I said. "Tulsa was fun for a while, and I love Aunt Eileen to death, but I got homesick."

"Maybe that's not as silly as it sounds, at this particular moment." Joanie leaned forward. "Johnny's home for the summer. Maybe you two can get back together."

My heart plummeted to my feet. I'd hoped against hope he'd spend the summer in Chicago where he belonged. I couldn't possibly face him, now or ever again.

I recognized Joanie's quizzical expression before she went on.

"I never did understand why you two broke up," she said in a calculating tone. "That's what happened, right? You broke up?"

I nodded uncomfortably. "That was just a kid thing," I said, my voice low and insincere. *Please, God, don't let him come looking for me.*

"Then you won't mind if I, uh…you know."

"Be my guest." She was going to make a play for Johnny after what he'd done to me? I bit my lip. She didn't know about all that had happened, and I prayed she never would.

"Thanks!" She took a final noisy slurp of her soda and hopped off her stool. "He was draggin' Main in his convertible last night with a couple of the guys. Maybe tonight he'll switch to girls."

She gave me a rakish wink and turned to leave, her hips swinging in one of those new short skirts—mini-skirts, the magazines were calling them. It looked kind of cheap to me, but it sure wouldn't take much fabric to make one.

Johnny. That was all over, as far as I was concerned. I hustled back to work, trying to put him entirely out of my mind.

An hour later, I could barely believe my eyes. That couldn't possibly be Johnny swinging through the front door, could it? I turned and rushed back to the kitchen where Mother hovered over the grill. She looked up, startled by my sudden entrance.

"It's Johnny," I said helplessly. "I don't want to talk to him."

"I don't blame you one bit." She handed me the

spatula. "Finish up these hamburgers and I'll take care of the front."

Glad to make the exchange, I took the spatula and did something Mother never allowed: I punched down hard on one of the burgers sizzling on the grill. It helped my frustration but didn't do the burger much good.

Mom cocked her head and smiled. "Give that squashed burger to Ron," she suggested. "That kid never knows what he's eating anyway."

I wanted to laugh, but my state of anxiety wouldn't permit it. I leaned over the grill and strained my ears but could hear nothing out front above the sizzle. Nor were my mother or Johnny in sight through the pass-through window.

Why had he come here, anyway? After the way he'd treated me, I was surprised he had the nerve to face me. He must be a completely different boy than I'd believed. Fool me once, shame on you. Fool me twice, shame on me.

A half hour or so later, Mother reentered the kitchen. "He's gone," she said.

"What did he want?"

She shrugged.

"Did he say anything about…about me?"

"He asked if he could talk to you and I said no."

"Is that all?"

"I told him if he ever came close to you again your brothers would mash him like a bug."

"Oh, Mom, you didn't say that!"

"I not only said it, I mean it. Stay away from him, honey. He's no good for you. You should know that by now."

I lifted my chin, feeling unfairly challenged in some way. "I *am* keeping away from him." And every other boy I knew. There wasn't one I'd trust as far as I could throw him. The only man I could count on was my father, who might be strict but at least he was honorable.

"That's my girl. You'll get over him, trust me. You'll meet some nice boy one of these days and forget there ever was a Johnny Davis."

"I hope so." But I doubted it.

Tossing my apron into the laundry basket on my way out for my break, I still hadn't gotten Johnny out of my mind. Grabbing my clutch purse off the rack, I slipped out the back door and came to an abrupt halt.

Johnny Davis straddled a rickety wooden chair, his chin resting on his arms, which were crossed over the chair's back. My gathered skirt swirled around my legs and my cheeks burned like fire. He'd waited all this time in the heat and humidity for me to come out? Damn him!

I had to admit he looked wonderful but somehow different. Older, thinner, stronger. Face lean, dark hair longer and in need of a trim. A college man, not a high-school boy.

But I wasn't a sophisticated college woman, I was just me, small-town girl, the same as I'd always been.

"What do you want?" I crossed my arms protectively over my chest and glared at him.

"Just to talk."

Same voice, low and vibrant. It never failed to send chills down my back.

"We have nothing to talk about," I informed him stiffly.

"You don't think so?"

"I know so. When the letters stopped—"

"Whose letters?" A quick flash of resentment colored his words.

"You know whose letters!"

"Don't blame me for what you—"

"Stop it." I shook my head stiffly. "It's over, whatever it was. Go away and leave me alone."

"Not until we get a few things straight."

Tears welled. I couldn't let him see me cry. "You broke my heart," I cried. "Now that I'm f-finally over you, you can't come in here digging up all that hurt again."

"That's not what I'm trying to do, Frankie. I'm trying to clear up whatever messed us up. Something happened and I don't know what it was."

Something happened, all right. Didn't he even wonder what had become of the baby? *Our* baby? He rose and started toward me. I let out a little shriek and took a step toward the door.

"Go back to Chicago," I cried. "You don't belong here, you…you foreigner!"

"Frankie, don't try to avoid the inevitable. I'm going to talk to you whether—"

I backed through the kitchen door and slammed it hard. Then I rested my forehead on the uneven wood surface and tried not to cry.

I HADN'T WANTED to talk to Johnny, but I didn't want him to leave town without even trying again. Just seeing him around, even from a distance, almost killed me. Having him value me so lightly was even worse.

Joanie was the one who told me Johnny was gone,

and she said it with a sigh. "He never even gave me a tumble," she mourned. "You were smart to dump him, Frankie."

Yeah, smart me.

Mother took one glance at me the day I ran into Johnny and sent me home halfway through my shift. "You look like you've lost your last friend," she said. "Either that or you're coming down with something."

"I'm okay," I lied halfheartedly, for he had been my best friend at one misguided time.

"Go home." She patted my cheek. "You've been working too hard. You deserve some time off."

Grateful, I took her up on the offer, walking the few blocks between Reva's and home. As I expected, no one else was there. That meant I could throw myself across my bed and scream and yell and cry until I got all of the frustration out of me, and him with it.

My brothers all had jobs and came home just long enough to eat, change clothes and take off again. Except for Jerry, the oldest, who'd married one of the Abenathy girls and had his own place now. He still dropped around occasionally for a decent meal.

In my room, I considered my options. Instead of a total breakdown, I should square my shoulders and look ahead, not backward.

I peeled off my cotton skirt and blouse and climbed into jeans and a gingham shirt. I rolled up the denim legs a bit, pulled up my shirttail and tied it in a knot, and smoothed my ponytail into some semblance of order. Humidity hung over me like a fog, but I didn't pay much attention. I'd lived here all my life, minus that stint in Oklahoma, which was just as bad when it came to humidity.

Of course, Aunt Eileen had air-conditioning. We should be so lucky here at home.

In the kitchen, I took a short bottle of grape soda out of the refrigerator and opened it with the church key hanging beside the windowsill. Maybe I'd find a good book and sit under one of the big old black walnut trees in the backyard and get him totally out of my—

I heard the squeak of the screen door and knew someone had just arrived home. The boys always headed straight for the kitchen so I waited for one of them to appear.

None did. Could it be Daddy, taking off from the store for lunch or something? On quiet bare feet, I moved toward the living room. I heard the low murmur of Daddy's voice and stopped outside the door. I couldn't see him but I could hear him.

"—can't, Millie. You shouldn't be calling here anyway."

Millie? Who was Millie? He couldn't be talking to widow Millicent Robberson, could he? Her daughter was a few years younger than me and a real snot. They lived outside town but I'd never been to their neighborhood.

A pause, then, "Honey, you know I want to, but Mary is dragging me to a card party tonight. Uh-huh…uh-huh…that'll work. Tomorrow night, then…"

This was weird. What could he be doing tomorrow night with Millicent Robberson? And calling her *honey,* yet.

"I love you, too, sweetheart." I'd never heard him speak in that low, intimate tone before, certainly not to my mother. "Put on those satin sheets and we'll have ourselves a big time—"

I dropped my pop bottle. Purple liquid exploded in an arc, leaving colorful spots on my feet, the wall and floor.

I heard Daddy yell, "What the hell!" and then the tramp of his feet. Too stunned to move, I kneeled and reached for the empty bottle, ignoring the sticky purple blotches everywhere.

"What the hell are you doing out here?" Daddy spit out the words while I hunkered down on the floor.

"I dropped my bottle of pop," I said. Stupid. He could see that.

"Were you spying on me?"

"I wouldn't do that, Daddy. Why would I? I—I didn't even know you were here. I came out of the kitchen and slipped on that throw rug you're always yelling about and dropped the bottle."

"Look, I'm gonna grab a sandwich and get back to work. You clean up this mess before your mother sees it, you hear?"

"I will, Daddy. Don't worry."

There was no need for him to worry. I'd be worrying enough for all of us.

Present

THE JERK AT the rear of the Jeep caught Frankie by complete surprise. She steered quickly to the shoulder, unable to see anything in the rearview mirror through the blowing sleet. Obviously some idiot had slammed a car into Myrna's Jeep. So much for Frankie's "I'm a safe driver" theory.

Crap. More delays. Hoping no serious damage had been done, she climbed out of the car and trudged back through the sting of ice chips to confront the maniac who had, in the words of her granddaughter, harshed her mellow.

Frankie exchanged phone numbers and insurance information with the smart-mouthed kid driver of the other car. The Jeep's bumper and the left rear fender were a bit banged up.

Formalities observed, she watched the kid speed away into the haze, another accident waiting to happen. Hands trembling, she started the Jeep and took a deep breath.

Time to get back on the road to St. Louis. Hang on, Johnny.

CHAPTER SEVEN

I COULDN'T TELL Mother about overhearing Daddy talking to his girlfriend. One minute I thought I should, the next I knew I couldn't. What would I say? How would she react? If she knew what he was doing, it would probably break up a long, and I thought mostly happy, marriage. I didn't want to be responsible for that.

But he was humiliating her. That grated on me because I'd been taken in, too. Was Mother really this blind? Where was her pride?

I began to watch Daddy more closely, though at first only half-consciously and then with more determination.

I noticed when he went out, when he came back, the smell of an unknown perfume from time to time, a pink feather in his jeans pocket that didn't come from anything my mother owned. How had I missed the clues for all those years? How had Mother?

Were all men, young or old, alike, as Daddy had told me once? Could any of them be trusted? My grief knew no boundaries, and yet I said nothing about my father's affair, not even to my friends. I would protect Mother, and me, by keeping my mouth closed.

I saw the man I trusted least of all only a few times before he burst back into town in the spring of 1967, and this time he was different. Johnny Davis left as a college kid and came back, to quote my father, as a "damned hippie."

I heard he was back but hadn't seen him yet and didn't want to, although my heart pounded wildly at just the mention of his name. There was plenty of talk about him around town. "He's just one of them damned hippies," I heard old Mrs. Kelly say. Since she was a well-known gossip, the only word that surprised me was the *damned*.

Others said even worse things—that he was probably a druggie by now, that he'd been kicked out of college, that his father was on the verge of disowning him.

Still, I must admit I was curious. I couldn't imagine Johnny as a hippie. To naive little me, the hippie life sounded kind of romantic. To run around with flowers in your hair, digging folk music and dancing in the streets. Wild and free they were, things I'd never been and wasn't sure I even wanted to be, but it was strangely engaging.

A few anxious days later a car pulled up beside me one afternoon as I walked home from the café. One glance revealed Johnny behind the wheel. He'd tied back his long, shaggy hair with a leather thong, and a brightly patterned T-shirt covered his broad shoulders.

He patted the back of the passenger seat and said, "Get in, babe."

My jaw must have been hanging open. I followed his order without thought, clutching my hands together in my lap and staring straight ahead, wondering why I was here when I hated him so.

He revved up the car and pulled away from the curb. "Where are we going?" I asked in a puny little voice.

"Someplace we can talk."

"I don't want to t-talk. What are you doing here anyway? Why aren't you at school?"

"I dropped out."

"Oh, Johnny, no! I heard you were kicked out, but—"

"The gossips got it wrong. I quit before they could get rid of me."

"Why?"

He abruptly swerved to the shoulder of the road and stopped the car. "Because I've got better things to do. I'm going to marry you, Frankie Hale, and take you away from all this. We're going to San Francisco and we're going to live our own lives without trying to please anybody but each other. We won't have to worry about money because my grandpa left me plenty." He glared at me. "Is that okay with you?"

"No, it isn't! I wouldn't marry you if you were the last man on earth." I screamed it at him, screamed it into the wind. "After the way you treated me, after you quit writing to me—"

"I didn't quit writing, you did!"

"Are you kidding? After my last letter you just cut me off."

"You mentioned that damned letter before. I've read it until the creases are tearing and I still don't know what the problem is. I *did* answer it. I answered all your letters, and then I wrote you a dozen more trying to find out what I'd done wrong and why you stopped answering."

While he spoke, he pulled out his wallet and extracted a baby-blue envelope. Then he carefully slid out several sheets of matching paper and began to recite the words without even looking at the pages.

"'Dear Johnny—how's school? I miss you so much! When will you be home again? I can hardly bear to walk down the streets without thinking of you driving up in your big convertible to take me for a ride. I remember all the things we said to each other before you left and—'"

I sobbed and my heart nearly bounded out of my chest. That certainly wasn't my final letter. Johnny looked at me in alarm.

"What's wrong?"

"That isn't the last letter I wrote you."

"It's sure as hell is the last letter I got."

"Something's very wrong here."

"You're shaking like a leaf. What was in the last letter?"

Oh, God, I couldn't tell him that *now,* not after what I'd done. Stammering, I tried to think of something to say.

He started to reach for me, then pulled me back against the car seat. "Was it about that trip to visit your aunt?"

"Who told you about that?"

"My mom."

"Who told her?"

"Your mom. I guess they're getting pretty tight."

What a horrible thought. Through my guilt and confusion, I fought to focus. "I needed to get away and Aunt Eileen invited me to Tulsa," I said. "I can't believe you kept writing to me."

"I sure as hell did."

"I didn't get any of your letters. That means…" *Let me mail it for you, honey. I need to get some more stamps.*

We stared at each other, horrified. I said one word— "Mother?"—and threw myself into his arms.

"MARRY ME." Johnny shifted around in the driver's seat to look straight into my eyes. He'd parked on the familiar bluff overlooking the creek, and for a minute, we'd been silent.

Now he leaned forward and said, "Let's get out of here and never come back."

I leaned into his arms and pressed my cheek beneath his chin, not saying a word.

His tone turned anxious. "Say something."

"Okay. I'll answer as soon as you say the magic words."

"And that would be…?"

"That would be *I love you*. That's what you should say first, before the proposal."

"You know I love you," he said. "You've always known that."

"I only hoped because I haven't been any too sure lately."

He groaned, his chest rising. "I never stopped loving you, even when it looked like we were washed up."

"I believe you." I straightened and cupped his face in my hands. "I love you so much it hurts, Johnny. Yes, I'll marry you and follow you anywhere."

He nuzzled the top of my head. "I'm sorry I got things in the wrong order. It's hard for me to say what I feel sometimes."

"I know that, but I need to hear it."

"I know you do. Frankie, I never heard my parents say they loved each other. I'm not sure I ever heard either of them say they loved *me*. Be patient, okay?"

"Okay." I kissed his throat. "It will get easier, honey. All it takes is practice. I'm glad we talked about this."

He nodded. "We need to have more faith in each

other and never let anyone come between us again. It's just you and me, babe. Just you and me.

"Now, let's make plans."

I nodded, heart in my throat. *Tell him, tell him now about the baby.* But this wasn't the right time. Later...

BY THE TIME I got home, I'd tucked away my joy and slipped into fury. Even then, I could hardly believe that my mother would do such a thing as lie to me the way she had. She'd never been the suspicious type, like Joanie's mom. My mother didn't snoop in my room, didn't open my mail before giving it to me, didn't question every move I made...or so I'd thought.

Maybe she was sneaky enough to say one thing and do another. If she told me today that she'd messed with Johnny's and my mail "for your own good," I wouldn't be responsible for my actions.

Johnny pulled the car to a stop at the curb. "I know you're dreading this. I'd be glad to go in with you."

"Not this time." I threw open the door and stepped out, pausing to straighten my clothes. "I have to do this on my own."

"I understand. I've got to go talk to my own mother about this, too, and I'm not looking forward to it, either. Just don't...say anything you'll regret."

"I'll try not to." I hesitated with a hand on the door. "When do you want to leave and where are we going?"

"Is tomorrow too soon?" He grinned. "We'll get married in Las Vegas."

I nodded. "I'll be ready." I blew him a kiss, my hand trembling. "Till then."

"It can't come soon enough."

He stayed there outside the house, waiting until I got

inside before driving away. When I stepped inside, Mother called from the kitchen.

"That you, Frankie?"

"Yes."

I walked into the kitchen and stopped just inside the door.

She took one look at me and said, "What's wrong?"

I drew a deep breath to steady myself. I'd never confronted my mother, or anyone else, about anything, but I couldn't stop now. I said bluntly, "You didn't mail my letter."

She frowned. "What letter?"

"My letter to Johnny. About the baby."

The color literally drained from her face. "Frankie—"

"Don't make it worse, Mother." My voice trembled with suppressed anger. "I know you didn't mail it because he never got it. You also kept his letters from me, and my guess is that his mother was doing the same. How could you be so cruel?"

"I did it for your own good, honey." She pressed her hands hard against the counter.

I let out a cry of incredulity. "I knew you'd say that! That's always your excuse—*for my own good.* You changed my entire life and Johnny's, too. I've been through *hell* about the baby and about losing Johnny."

"I never intended to cause you—"

"Stop it! You intended to keep us apart, and you did, but that's over. Johnny and I have cleared everything up and we're leaving here tomorrow. We're going to—"

"No!" Tears ran down her cheeks. "Frankie, you're too young, both of you. How will he support you?"

"As if that matters. The fact is, his grandfather left him money."

"So then he'll be a lazy bum living off the money somebody else made? Don't you see—"

"Why do you hate him so much? He's wonderful."

"I don't hate him, not at all. Maybe later when you're both older—"

I felt sorry for her, but not sorry enough to stop. "Who says you're so wonderful at picking out good husband material? You didn't do such a great job for yourself. Did Grandma approve of Daddy? Did she tell you to stick to him no matter what?"

Her forehead wrinkled in a frown. "I…I don't understand what you're getting at."

"His girlfriends, Mother. Millie what's her name, and who knows how many others? I've found things in his pockets that didn't come from you. Perfume that isn't yours on his collar."

"Oh, God."

Her shoulders slumped and she covered her face with her hands. I couldn't tell if she was crying, but I felt lower than a snake's belly, as my brothers would have said. I'd gotten even, but in such a horrible, vindictive way.

I took a guilty step forward. "I'm sorry. I shouldn't have told you. I know it's a shock but—"

Her hands fell away from her face. "The only shock is that you know," she said in a dead voice. "How did you find out?"

"I accidentally overheard a phone call between him and that Millie person. That opened my eyes and I started seeing things I'd never noticed before. I didn't dream you already knew."

"I've known for a long time."

"And you just went on as if everything was all right? How could you do that?"

"It hasn't been easy, especially at first." She slumped against the counter, fingers spread wide. "I had a life I liked. I had—still have a family to protect, Frankie. He kept…kept trying to do better."

"But cheating on you—" My mouth turned down in censure. "How could you put up with that and keep your…your *pride?*"

"Pride had little to do with it." She lifted her head and looked me straight in the eye. "I love your father, Frankie. He was the only boyfriend I ever had. I knew the minute I met him that he was the one."

"Like me and Johnny?" I could hardly believe what she was saying.

She nodded. "As I got older and, I hope, wiser, I wondered so many times if I'd done the right thing getting married so young. I don't think he'd had time to…to sow his wild oats. But looking back, I've never met another man more interesting to me than your father."

"After what he did—what he's doing—you still feel that way?"

"I made a choice, a choice I hope you never have to make. It's one of the main reasons I want you to slow down long enough to grow up."

She drew a shaky breath. "I can't tell you how many hours your father and I spent talking about this. He makes promises…he tries…" Her voice trailed away. "I pretend to believe him because I *want* to believe. As long as no one confronted me about it—"

"Like I'm doing."

"Yes. Up until now, I didn't have to make a choice. I could just let it ride and hope for the best."

"I don't want to hear any more." I shook my head in disappointment. "Daddy's *your* problem. My problem is that you betrayed me—my own mother. I'm leaving tomorrow and that's that."

"I know I can't stop you, but—"

"That's right, you can't. I won't say a word about this conversation to anyone, Mother, and I expect you won't say anything about the missing letter and what it contained."

"I didn't read it. I just…put it aside in a safe place."

"Then burn it," I said flatly, not believing for a single second that she hadn't opened it. I'd find it difficult to believe anything she said to me from this point on. I turned away. "I think this discussion is over."

"No, Frankie, it isn't. There's so much more to say."

"Maybe, but not today. Not today." I walked out of the room, feeling as if I were in charge for the first time in my life. I'd learned so many awful things today, but also some wonderful things.

It seemed as if I had to pay for everything.

I CALLED JOHNNY later and the first thing I heard was his mother's angry voice in the background. "You told her what we're doing," I said.

"Yeah. Look, I can't talk with her here. She's talking in my other ear. Wanna go out for a soda?"

"Good idea. I'm not feeling too good around here, either."

He arrived within a half hour and drove us to the Dairy Queen drive-in. Bev Olsen took our order and I noticed her check out Johnny.

When the drinks came, she leaned forward and said to him, "I hear you've turned into a bad boy."

"You shouldn't believe everything you hear."

She laughed, not easy when simultaneously batting her eyelashes. "Looking at you, I think it's true."

He smiled, handed me my drink and took my hand in his. Bev shrugged and sashayed back to pick up the next order.

"So how did it go with your mother?"

"Bad." He stared through the windshield for a moment. "You're not going to believe me but she said she—"

"Did it for your own good?"

"Jeez, were you there?"

"No. It's what my mother said, what she always says." My shoulders slumped. "Your mother doesn't like me, does she?"

"No, but it has nothing to do with you personally. She's picked out a girl for me in Chicago and just won't give up the idea. She wouldn't like any girl I got interested in around here."

"My mother just thinks we're too young."

"Ditto."

"I hope we're not," I said. "Too young, I mean."

"Age has nothing to do with it," he said with complete conviction, "so long as we stick together and work out our problems. There are very few things that are unforgivable."

Things like giving away a baby are unforgivable, I thought. He could never forgive me for that, as I could never forgive cheating.

CHAPTER EIGHT

I TOSSED A STACK OF underwear into my suitcase and took a final look around my bedroom. Johnny waited for me out front and I was going to him as soon as I threw just a few more things together.

My mother hovered near the bed, her face red and shiny with tears. "Don't do this, Frankie," she pleaded for the fortieth time. "We can work this out. You don't have to run away."

"I'm not running away. I'm leaving with the man I love—the *man,* Mother. He's not a boy anymore and I'm not a girl. I'm going with him no matter where he takes me."

"I don't suppose there's any point in me going over the same ground—"

"None at all. I'm nineteen. I'm an adult. Even if I wasn't, I wouldn't stay here after all that's happened."

I closed the suitcase, drained of emotion and less than interested in shoving anything else inside. "I'm taking my sewing machine."

"I don't care about your sewing machine. I care about *you.* You're going to be miserable."

"What is that? A self-fulfilling prophecy? You're wrong. My mind is made up and nothing will change it."

I turned to face her squarely. "Mother, I love you,

but at the moment I don't like you very much. When Johnny and I have our tenth wedding anniversary, maybe you'll admit you were wrong and we can start over. But trust me—I'll never let you touch one of my letters again." I picked up the suitcase with one hand and the sewing-machine handle with the other.

I had never felt such total distance from my mother. Deep down, I knew I was right and she was wrong in trying to keep me away from the man for whom I was fated. I *knew.*

Add to that the fact that she lived with a man who betrayed her time and again. I'd never understand how she could do that, or why he would do what he did.

"Don't worry about me," I said. "I'm going to be happy, happier than I've ever been in my life."

"You'll phone?"

"Or write. You'll hear from me one way or the other. Eventually." I picked up my burdens and walked away from what used to be my life.

I was heading for happiness, feeling superior to those who'd settled for less.

JOHNNY POINTED the car west, and I could hardly believe it was happening. I couldn't stop talking, couldn't calm down. Then when I finally did, I felt my eyes unexpectedly tear up.

Johnny glanced at me. "What's wrong, sweetheart? Are you sorry?"

I swallowed hard and dashed a hand across my damp cheeks. "Not about us. About my mother. I've never had this kind of a fight with her before."

"You'll make up. You're not leaving her forever."

"I know, but—" I stared at passing farm fields, colored with spring green. "I said some awful things to her."

"Things you didn't mean?"

I shook my head. "I meant every word but some of it was cruel."

"Will she forgive me for taking you away?"

"Yes." I didn't even have to think about that.

"Will you forgive her?"

I considered. Ultimately, everything with the baby had come out all right, but I'd gone through all those months of agony and despair, losing my son in the process. Then my mother had deceived me about my father, and he had deceived the whole family. Even so... "Yes," I said with a sigh. "I'll forgive her."

"Then call her when we get to California. You can work it out once you've had some time to think."

Of course we could.

JOHNNY AND I spent that first night in an old motel in some small town in Kansas. Nervous as a cat, I waited in the car while Johnny checked us into the garish establishment with its flashing lights and barren flower beds.

"Did they suspect anything?" I asked as we hauled our bags into the room.

He laughed. "What's to suspect? I registered us as Mr. and Mrs. Davis, which we will be as soon as we reach Las Vegas tomorrow. How do you like the sound of that?"

"I like it a lot," I said.

He took my bag and pointed me toward the focal point of the shabby room. "See that? That's a bed."

"I know a bed when I see one!"

'But that bed is different. That bed is *our* bed. I don't know about you but I've looked forward to this moment for a long, long time."

"Me, too." I barely whispered the words and my cheeks grew warm. It seemed so sinful to stare longingly at a bed when we weren't *really* married. A real bed made everything so official.

Too late to worry about *that*.

He steered me forward. "Let's stop wasting time and see if it works," he murmured in my ear. "Frankie, this is just the beginning of our life together so let's begin it right."

He was learning fast. He lifted me off my feet and I gasped and reached for him. Before I could grab hold he tossed me onto the bed. He joined me there, laughing, pulling me into his arms.

I went willingly, and soon I realized how right he was beds really were better than the backseat of a car or a blanket on the ground.

WE LAY ENTWINED, exhausted, breathing hard, and happy, happy, happy. Through the creases of the venetian blinds I could see the orange flash of the motel sign ..Happy Inn. That made me giggle. The place might be shabby but the name fit. I was truly happy.

I turned to press my body against his beneath the sheet, flimsy from many washings. "I can't believe we're really here," I said. "A week ago I thought it was all over between us."

"I never thought that." He slid his hand down my backbone, making me shiver. "I always knew it was you for me, Frankie."

"How could you be sure?"

"I felt it. Didn't you?"

"Yes, but it could have been one of those kid things."

"But it wasn't. What's wrong with you, girl? Don't you believe we were meant for each other?"

"I believe."

He curved a hand over my hip and squeezed gently. "Are you still worried about us, that this isn't the real thing?"

"God, no. I'm sure about me but…it just seems too good to be true, that you feel the same. Your background is so different."

He grew still. "My background is crummy," he said at last. "I have two parents who got married for all the wrong reasons, not at all like your mom and dad." His chest moved beneath my chin with the force of a deep breath. "Mom got pregnant with me. They don't realize I know that, but I came across their marriage license a few years back and it told me a lot."

"I'm sorry." I caressed his cheek, completely taken aback. "It's hard to believe our parents were ever really young and impulsive."

"You mean like us?"

I had to laugh with him. "Exactly like us. I suppose that's why they're so hard on us, because they're afraid we'll do the same things they did."

"Which we pretty much do." He leaned over me, his face shadowed. "Do you mind leaving your hometown to go someplace completely new and strange?"

"Not if I'm with you."

"You'll stick with me, no matter what?"

"Of course. I love you, Johnny. I'm yours and you're mine."

"That's how I feel. Honey, I'm taking you to a place

like none you've ever seen before. It offers a freedom that will blow your mind. Everybody does exactly what they want, when they want. It's a place of kindness and understanding and love, no judgments at all. You do your thing, they do theirs."

"That sounds kind of...scary. Why do you want this, Johnny?"

He bent his elbows and cradled his head in his hands. Looking up at the ceiling, he said, "I suppose I'm trying to rebel, like everyone else. I grew up with a lot of heavy expectations. Nobody asked what *I* wanted, they told me. Someday I'll probably want to go back and take over the family business just like they want me to, but for now...no way. All I want is you and a chance to get lost in the crowd for once."

He rolled over and draped one leg across me. I stroked his thigh, still astonished that I had the right to do that.

"We're young," I said, "and free. I suppose now is the time to experiment and find out what's really important to us. Besides each other, I mean."

"That's right. But don't you worry, Frankie. I'll always watch out for you. Our life will seem strange at first, but you'll catch on. Nobody judges. Nobody cares what you do. Everybody's doing their own thing and trying to create a new society free of the establishment."

I had no idea what the "establishment" might be, but that wasn't important right now. "What's the name of this place we're going to?" I asked him.

"The Haight." He kissed my throat and I felt the flick of his tongue. "We're going to Haight-Ashbury."

IN MY ENTIRE LIFE, I'd never been west of Kansas, so I found driving through the desert toward Las Vegas fascinating. The colors and shapes astonished me, as did the dryness of the heat. Johnny watched my delight with a smile, enjoying my excitement.

And Las Vegas! I'd never seen anything like it, especially the Strip, as Johnny called it. I'd never imagined such huge hotels and casinos with equally enormous signs flashing with light and movement, the press of cars on the streets and pedestrians on the sidewalks. Everyone seemed happy to be here, even in the heat, but not as happy as I was.

Johnny pulled into the Sands Hotel and gave me a cocky grin. "Let's stay here," he said. "I've got to make up for last night's accommodations."

I smiled back at him. "Hey, I had no problem with the Happy Inn."

"Trust me, you'll like it here more. Once we say our I-do's you'll never get away from me."

"I'll never want to," I said, meaning it from the bottom of my heart.

Married! I could hardly believe my dream was about to come true. Johnny took care of everything—the license, the chapel, even my new outfit.

He sent me shopping with a purse full of money and instructions to "buy something white," even though I protested. I didn't really rate white under the circumstances, but was too embarrassed to argue at length.

To please him, I chose a white brocade suit with a short fitted jacket, fitted skirt and white satin heels. I pulled my hair up into a French twist and took great care with what little makeup I used—lipstick and mascara.

Johnny approved, which was all I needed.

The ceremony itself passed in a blur. The only thing that sank in was Johnny, looking tall and handsome in a dark suit and fresh haircut. When he pulled out two gold wedding bands, I laughed out loud. I'd forgotten all about the rings.

Back at the Sands, he led me toward the elevators, his hand gripping mine. I followed, still in my daze. I only belatedly became aware of shouting from the direction of the gaming tables.

"You SOB, I'm gonna break both your legs!" somebody yelled.

I saw a short, slender man give a dealer a shove. "Do you know who I am?" he roared.

"Sir, there's nothing I can do. Your casino card is cut off. If you'll see the credit manager—"

"Screw the credit manager!"

The furious man continued to shout curses as he turned and stomped away from the argument, coming in our direction with a flock of men behind him. I pressed back against Johnny, wondering why he just stood there like a statue and stared.

The man with the bad language stopped short in front of us, his companions fanning out behind him. All of them glared at us with hard eyes.

Then the face of the man in charge softened. He had an attractive face, really, although not traditionally handsome. "What you doin' here, doll?" he asked.

"I—I—" I glanced helplessly at Johnny for assistance.

He said, "We just got married, sir."

"On purpose?" His goons snickered. "You and Elvis. He got married in this burg not long ago, but yours will probably last longer than his." He glanced back at his entourage and added, "Even if it's only six months."

Johnny said firmly, "Ours will last forever."

The man doing the talking tossed a snort over his shoulder. "They're kids. They'll learn." To me he said, "What's your name, babe?"

"F-Frankie."

"Hey, we got a name in common." He reached into his pocket, then extended his hand toward me and said, "Well? Take your wedding present."

Still mystified, I held out my hand and he dropped something in it—a silver dollar that clinked against the back of my new wedding ring.

"They're robbing me blind so that's about all I've got left," he said wrathfully. "Take this for good luck and have a happy life." The last two words seemed to take special effort to get out of his mouth. "If your game folds, toss it out the window of a fast-moving car."

Whipping around, he headed across the room toward the elevator, his mob at his heels. "We're moving to Caesar's," he roared. "They screwed with me here for the last time—"

I just stood there, holding the big silver coin. "Who *was* that?" I asked Johnny. "I hate to take his last dollar." I held out my hand to show my new husband the coin.

He burst out laughing and picked up the dollar. "Honey, you just got a wedding present from Ol' Blue Eyes," he said, flipping the silver disk into the air and catching it deftly. "I'm gonna put this buck away in a safe place and we'll pull it out on anniversaries and tell everyone the story of how we got it."

I smiled and nodded, but it was years later before I realized who'd given me that "gift."

WE WENT TO SEVERAL shows over the next couple of days, reveled in the luxury of our hotel suite and greatly enjoyed the enormous bed where we spent much of our time. The shows were good, I guess, but they showed a lot of semi-naked girls, which embarrassed me. Johnny had the decency not to call me a hick, but that's how I felt.

I wasn't unhappy when we pulled out of Las Vegas, heading west again. Johnny laughed at me and said I'd probably never been outside Missouri before this trip, which wasn't entirely true. I'd been to Chicago once and to Tulsa several times, not to mention Oklahoma City and Kansas City. Now there'd always be Las Vegas...

Still, San Francisco, which he and everyone else seemed to call The City, scared me to death.

So many people, so many cars, so many hills... What were we getting into? But then I looked at the man I loved and my faith and confidence returned.

Don't be silly, I scolded myself. He'll take care of me. We have love and we have money. I still didn't understand why he wanted to be a hippie but I was game.

We also had a place to live, what he described as a "small apartment right in the heart of the action." When he pulled to the curb in front of a towering, aging house sagging on its haunches, I caught my breath and stared.

Gray and weather-beaten, the building sprawled over a vivid landscape of flowers and vines, all enclosed behind a rusted iron fence with an open space where once a gate must have been.

Johnny jumped out of the car and started grabbing suitcases and packages from the backseat, all eager to get inside. I followed more slowly, insecure and overwhelmed again.

The front door hung open and we walked inside. Stairs rose on our right, a dingy hallway opened to our left. Johnny took the stairs two at a time.

"Hurry up, Frankie! We're home!"

Home? I swallowed hard and followed, stepping over a wad of cloth on the third step—a pair of jeans? And a few steps higher, a pair of women's underpants. And dirt and food wrappers and cobwebs everywhere.

My God, what was this place? I wasn't a snob, I assured myself, and I could live anywhere with my new husband, but this building reeked of abuse.

At the top of the gloomy stairs, Johnny turned right and kicked open a door. Unwilling to be left alone in this place, I scurried after him and then stopped short.

Outlined against light streaming through a huge window with sagging sheers stood a woman, or maybe a girl, wearing some kind of flowing blouse that concealed her body as efficiently as cellophane. I could see everything, her breasts and nipples clearly outlined by the backlight.

"Johnny!" The girl dropped some bright fabric onto the bed and rushed toward him, squealing with delight. Long curly hair swirled behind her. He dropped our belongings and met her with equal enthusiasm.

I stood there like a fifth wheel, with no idea what was going on. A deep, unfamiliar voice startled me from behind. "Is this her?"

I turned just in time to be swept into the arms of a stranger. He hugged me so tightly I couldn't get my breath to scream for help—and I would have, too.

He set me back on my feet and grinned at me, then

at Johnny. "Welcome home," he said. "Me and Lise fixed you up one cool pad."

"I tie-dyed your sheets!" Lise ducked away from Johnny and grabbed up the mound of red and pink and yellow fabric, wafting it into the air to settle it atop the bed. "Cool, huh?"

"Way cool," Johnny agreed. He turned to me, standing there stock-still and stunned. He looked just a tad doubtful himself when he saw me. "This is my wife, Frankie," he announced. "Honey, the chick is Lise and the clod who grabbed you is Ben-Boy."

Lise let out her breath in a hiss. "You *married* her?"

"Of course. I told you I would."

Ben-Boy beamed and said, "Peace," holding out his right hand with the first two fingers extended in a *V*. "How'd your old man dig your hookup?" He indicated the two of us with wiggling fingers. "Cut off all your bread?"

"It's not a hookup, it's a marriage. And I don't give a shit how he took it." Johnny looked annoyed at their lack of enthusiasm. "I don't need any bread from my folks, either. My grandpa left me all we need."

Ben-Boy said an envious, "Ah, so…"

At the moment, I was much more interested in staring at Ben-Boy than in the conversation. I'd seen pictures of hippies, but never in my life had I laid eyes on a human being dressed like this guy.

A dingy and ragged tie-dyed T-shirt hugged his chest and hung over the rattiest pair of holey jeans ever to grace a body. Bare toes dug into the rough wooden floor and he'd wrapped a swath of raw-edged red fabric about his long, ragged hair. A droopy mustache and unshaven chin completed the picture.

Lise flashed another peace sign and grinned. She wore no makeup and her hair presented a mad tangle. Along with her see-through blouse, she wore an ankle-length skirt of an equally gauzy material, and her beaded headband sported several droopy daisies.

She saw me staring. "Flower child," she said, pointing to the daisies. For the first time, I noticed a certain wobbly sound to her voice, and saw the way she kept licking her lips. "I brought some for you."

She pointed to the scarred wooden table. Several daisies drooped over the sides of a fruit jar. She raised a brow. "You didn't dress for it."

I sure didn't. I wore pressed jeans with a side zipper and a white blouse neatly tucked in, my hair in its usual ponytail.

Ben-Boy said, "We cleaned up to make a good impression on your chick."

I almost laughed aloud. Spiderwebs hung in the corners and dust bunnies adorned chair legs. A stack of dirty dishes towered out of the sink. Nevertheless, I thanked them very politely. Mother would have been proud. If she wouldn't have already fainted.

Lise sidled up to Johnny. "Wanna come hear the sounds with us tonight at the panhandle in Golden Gate? Lots of good stuff floating around."

Johnny looked straight at me. "Not tonight. We gotta get settled."

"Square." She drew one in the air with forefingers.

"Sorry. Anything happen while I was gone?"

She shrugged. "Nothing too much. Uh…you probably don't know about Slim."

"What happened to him?"

Lise and Ben-Boy exchanged quick glances.

"Bad trip. Real bad trip," said Ben-Boy.

"Did he—"

"Nah, but they locked him up after he went ape shit on the trolley. Threw out everybody, even the driver."

None of this made sense to me and I looked at Johnny questioningly. He shook his head and mouthed *Later,* then shooed his friends out.

At the door, Ben-Boy paused, holding out a cupped hand. "Gotta goody for you. You'll dig it. Way groovy."

"Not now," Johnny said. "Easy, man."

"Easy?" Ben-Boy glanced at me and nodded in understanding. "Cute chick but not real cool."

And that's how I met my first hippies.

CHAPTER NINE

ONCE EVERYBODY except me and Johnny left the house, I called my mother.

"I'm sorry," I said in a choked voice. "I shouldn't have talked to you that way, but I was so upset."

"Don't worry, sweetheart." Her voice also sounded thick with emotion. "I'm so relieved to hear from you, to know that you're all right."

"I'm fine." I spared a glance to my surroundings, which would have made her pass out. "I'm Mrs. Johnny Davis, Mother. We got married in Las Vegas."

"I—I'm happy for both of you." She cleared her throat. "And Daddy's accepted it, too. Just remember, you can always come back home—both of you, I mean. Give Johnny my love and welcome him to the family. And to you, baby, always my love to you."

I hung up, relieved, and faced the problems at hand. Time and elbow grease, I assured myself, would pay off for me in the end.

I ADMITTED TO MYSELF, but not to Johnny, that my first reaction to our so-called apartment, not to mention Johnny's friends, was shock. Nevertheless, I pulled myself together and searched for the bright side. I could do lots of things to make this place more homey, not to mention cleaner. Anybody comfortable here the way it was now must have been born in a barn.

Johnny left decorating up to me, but he watched with some anxiety. "You don't like it here, do you?" he said after the first couple of days. He looked so crestfallen that I couldn't stand it.

"Don't worry, Johnny," I said. "Now that I've almost got this place cleaned—"

"You're working too hard. We can move if you want to."

"I'm not working too hard! I hate sitting around." I thought about the rest of his comment. "You like it here, with your friends nearby," I said at last. "I don't know why, really—"

"This is where it's at," he broke in, taking my hands in his. "Ben-Boy was my roommate at Berkeley and I got to coming here after he dropped out of school and moved into this building. It's a free society here, Frankie. Make love, not war. Life is about being happy, about wanting a better world."

And drugs, I thought. I'd already seen enough to know people didn't get this "happy" without pharmaceutical help.

He sighed. "I'm not all that wrapped up in the 'better world' thing. But damn! I've been so friggin' 'good' all my life, just like you have. I want to break loose for once, see how it feels, don't you? Then we can go back and be responsible adults, or go crazy somewhere else. Just not quite yet...unless it's making you nuts."

"No, honey." I put my arms around him. "I love you and want you to be happy."

I really did. He was my entire world, my friend and

my lover. I could stay here. It wouldn't be for long. I could stand anything for a little while.

All that really interested him about our apartment was the bed, which I thought was sagging and creaky and covered with mind-altering colors. Fortunately for me, it broke the third night we spent in it, sending us crashing to the floor in a convulsion of giggles while still tightly entwined.

"You guys all right?" Someone started pounding on the door.

"Cool, man!" Johnny could barely get the words out, he was laughing so hard.

He bought us a new bed the next day, but I kept the psychedelic sheets. I'd never want to hurt Lise's feelings.

With the apartment sparkling clean, I went to work on the decorations, if they could be called such. Down came the dreary and dust-encrusted window sheers of some unknown original color. In their place I put up crisp white curtains with blue borders, stitched quickly on my trusty sewing machine. I added ruffled toppers and stood back to admire my work.

The windows gleamed; the curtains fell in graceful folds. The sight filled me with satisfaction.

Johnny never even noticed but Lise did.

"What's coming off here?" she demanded, staring at my curtains.

I suggested tentatively, "Dirt?"

She frowned. "Johnny told us to cool it with you, but I never thought…"

She'd really lost me. "Thought what?"

"That you'd be this stupid white-bread establishment." The words sounded scornful, as was the glance she gave me.

The last thing I wanted was to get into a hassle with this woman, even if she did wear ragged blue jeans with peace signs painted on the legs and tight T-shirts that showed everything she had, which was plenty.

"I am what I am," I said, dodging conflict. "How about a nice cold glass of lemonade?" Anything to soothe her. "Let's sit down so we can talk."

"Lemonade?" She grimaced. "You got any pot?"

"The bathroom is—"

"Not *a* pot! Pot! Mary Jane, weed—"

It dawned on me but slowly. "Do you mean dope?"

"Dope!"

"My mother always called that stuff 'dope' because you have to be a dope to use it." I held out a frosty glass of lemonade. By this point, I didn't care if I offended her or not. My voice hardened. "Sit down and drink."

She did, her look rebellious, and I wondered why. She didn't know me. We'd lived here for only four months or so. Why take my orders?

Unless that was what drugs did to you. "I don't understand this town," I said. "I don't understand you or Ben-Boy or the bums I see huddled in doorways with too much hair and dirt and not enough sense to come in out of the rain."

"It doesn't rain in California."

"Tell me why, Lise."

Sparks flared in her eyes. "You don't know shit about what's going on, do you?"

I shook my head.

She drew in a deep scornful breath. "We're here to get away from the greedy materialism of the establishment. We support what's good. We protest the Vietnam war and rally for civil rights. We fight against the white man's perverted society of pollution and gluttony—"

"You're white." Under the dirt, anyway.

"I deny that. I'm a citizen of the world, no-color waiting for the light."

You're a dingbat waiting to die if you keep this up. "How do you live? You still need money."

"Money." Her lips turned down at the corners. "We do some begging, until the pigs show up and hassle us. Johnny gives us bread when we're in a pinch, and sometimes we hook a stash from some downie. And we party…blow our minds where you sads can never go."

"Oh, Lise, that's not a real life. I've already seen what happens—"

"You've seen nothing. Not a damned thing. You're here in your little hole wiggin' out over *curtains.*" She finished the last drop of her drink and stood, pressing red knuckles against the tabletop. Was hand lotion unknown to her?

She sneered at me. "How did Johnny get mixed up with a coconut like you? I thought he'd bring me a sister and instead I get *you,* square as a concrete block."

I laughed. "Are you insulting me? In what language?"

"Go ahead, snicker. But I know now that Johnny's up for grabs, because you're not near enough for him. What I plan to do to him will make him forget you even exist."

Suddenly the fun was gone. "Stop it. You stay away from him."

"You gonna make me?" She glanced around, her lip curled. "This is a bad scene. I'm out of here."

I stood there for a few minutes, staring at the door.

I didn't like the sound of that *at all*. But Johnny would never...

I refilled my glass and walked to the window, which overlooked the street. Ben-Boy said pilgrims were flooding in, taking space they didn't deserve away from the regulars. Masses of people passed below in an endless swirl of color and motion.

I already knew that I belonged in the Haight like Lise belonged at a society tea party. I looked different, I acted different, I understood nothing.

But I loved my husband. So I kept trying and trying and trying, if not to fit in, at least not to fit *out* so obviously. I got a little messy, stopped ironing my jeans, wore my shirt untucked, tried to look hip.

That was a laugh.

Johnny watched me with some anxiety. He wanted me to be content, and I was—with him. When we were together we laughed and played and came to know each other on far deeper levels. Without him, I was what my mother called a gone gosling.

Often we went to concerts of music I didn't like, and people did things I didn't want to see—drugs and sex, mostly. At picnics the dancers threw off their clothes and danced around like idiots, at parties the only two sober and completely clothed people in the room were us.

Time passed, Thanksgiving and Christmas all but ignored except for the gifts from my family. Johnny seemed content, but I kept trying to figure out what this meant to him. He seemed genuinely intrigued by the goings-on. Had he done drugs before I arrived? He said no, except for pot a few unsuccessful times, and so did Ben-Boy. I never bothered to ask Lise. I wouldn't have believed her anyway.

Never once did Johnny show any interest or tendencies toward drugs. It never occurred to me that he ever would.

I do think the changes in our apartment overwhelmed him, unfortunately. Nobody else lived in a clean pad with matching curtains and tablecloths, painted-to-match furniture—though it was old and shabby—and had home-cooked meals, and a hostess decked out in crisp, colorful cottons with matching ribbons and headbands while at home.

I'd see them trace "square" with their fingers like Lise did and roll their eyes when they saw me, but everyone liked Johnny so much that they didn't hassle me. On my part, I regretted their disapproval, but the day I put on ragged jeans and a tie-dyed T-shirt, minus a bra, would be one cold day in hell. Unpressed jeans were as far as I could go.

THEN ONE DAY, Johnny came home from some excursion with Ben-Boy sporting that glazed expression I'd grown used to seeing on others. My heart stopped beating and my stomach dropped.

Johnny looked at me, stifled a giggle, went straight to the refrigerator and I knew. Lise and Ben-Boy giggled and ate everything they could find when they did pot. God, I was starting to think the way they did.

"It's no big thing," he said, trying to soothe me. "A little weed never hurt anybody. It's better for me than tobacco."

"Neither is good for you," I pleaded against his shoulder in disappointment. "It's dope, just like all the other stuff people around here jam into their bodies. Please don't do it again, Johnny. Promise me you won't do pot ever again."

His sigh sent a shudder through his body. "I won't, Frankie. If it hurts you this much, I won't."

It never occurred to me to mention any of the other drugs—acid, cocaine… In fact, I didn't know much about other drugs, just that hippies used them and I didn't consider Johnny, my beloved Johnny, to be a real, true hippie. I'd overheard a black dude call Johnny "a white boy trying to be cool," and maybe he was.

I thought of him as disappointed in his family and his previous world—the establishment—and felt confident that this would all pass. Then we'd return to our previous lives.

This current spell was no more than a bump in the road, because he was young and breaking loose. As long as I was with him, we'd be okay.

Unfortunately, I'd overlooked the true meaning of a popular hippie cry: sex, drugs and rock 'n' roll.

WE BOTH TRIED really hard to make the best of the situation, which created its own tensions.

Johnny gave me more attention, as if trying to make up for his marijuana slip, and I made it a point to go out with him as often as I could stand.

I saw things in Haight-Ashbury that no normal person should have to look at. Drunks and druggies sprawled in doorways, naked and near-naked hippies of all sexes—when I thought there were only two—cavorting in public, having sex. They'd put nickels in parking meters, spread their blankets and sit there silently meditating or tripping until their time ran out. They sang and did drugs and danced around, flinging off what little clothing they wore.

Was I shocked? You better believe it.

These sights embarrassed Johnny because of me, and he tried to steer clear of such spectacles for my sake. Considering our address, not much could be done. Especially at the concerts, which were noise and nothing else to me.

When Johnny tried to talk me into going to Golden Gate to hear the Grateful Dead one more time, I shuddered at the thought.

"Stay here," I countered. "Please. Those concerts are getting awfully rough. Why don't we go out for a nice dinner somewhere? You keep promising to take me to Chinatown."

Lise walked in about then, knocking apparently unknown to her. "Come with Ben-Boy and me," she urged Johnny, placing a plate of something brown that might be chocolate on the table. "I'll just leave these brownies here for your darling Frankie, who never wants to go anywhere or do anything anyway."

She batted her eyelashes at me and smiled, a real breakthrough if it hadn't been so cold. "I remember you saying the other night how much you like anything chocolate. Ben-Boy does, too."

I feared my smile in return was strained. I just couldn't warm up to Lise and I knew she didn't like me, either. For the guys, we tried to keep up a friendly pretense, but I'd sooner leave than eat her brownies.

"Thanks," I said. "That's very nice of you."

She shrugged her peasant-blouse-covered shoulder, the sheer fabric clearly revealing her nipples, as usual. She didn't care about me, just Johnny.

"Frankie, I really want to go," Johnny said. "Why don't you come along? We'll have a good time."

"A good time, getting pushed around by the crowd

and hassled by the police? I don't think so. Let's go out to eat, Johnny. Please?"

"I don't know…" He wavered.

Ben-Boy stuck his head into the room. "Let's get a move on. We gotta bash to go to."

Lise looked at him with raised eyebrows. "Not gonna tell them?"

Ben shrugged and walked into the room, his expression turning glum. "You're bringing me down, chick."

Lise said to us, "They finally caught up with him."

Johnny looked as confused as I was. "Who?"

"The lottery," Ben-Boy glumly. "I'm heading to Canada, maybe tomorrow if you got bread I can bum off you."

Still confused, I said, "The lottery?"

"Draft lottery," Johnny explained. "That's a real bummer, man."

"Don't I know it." Ben-Boy actually drooped.

Astounded, I stared at him. "You're going to be a draft dodger?"

"And proud of it," Lise added, sensing my strong disapproval.

"One of Frankie's brothers just enlisted," Johnny said. "He didn't want to mess around waiting for his number to come up."

I nodded, proud of his patriotism. Where I came from, all men went into the military service at one point or the other, it seemed. My father fought in WWII and I was proud of him for that…but little else. My mother, however, had taught me to be polite no matter how hard it was and I held my tongue.

I could afford to be charitable. Johnny would never run. If his draft notice came, he'd do his duty.

"I tried the Four-F route," Ben-Boy said plaintively. "They didn't take me for a conscientious objector, either. I got no choice but to scram."

"So in the meantime," Lise said, all cheerful anticipation, "we'll get the groove on tonight—big going-away party for the boy, here."

Everybody but me smiled.

Johnny turned to me and his smile disappeared. "Will you come for Ben-Boy?"

"If I won't go for you, do you think I'd go for him? I hate those scenes. They're an invitation for disaster."

"I'm sorry you feel that way." He headed for the door, and Lise linked her arm with his as he passed.

Ben-Boy looked at all of us, frowning. "Frankie? Be a sport, chick. It'll be a blast."

I turned my back on him. "I don't like blasts," I said. "And I see no need to celebrate you running away to Canada like a—" I stopped short. Who was I to judge him? I looked at them. "Be careful," I said, and that was my final, silly advice.

CHAPTER TEN

I SHOULDN'T HAVE touched those brownies but I did. I was anxious and angry enough that I wasn't paying attention and didn't even remember picking one up. To my surprise, I found myself with a mouthful of surprisingly tasty chocolate, which filled me with astonishment that Lise could really *bake*.

I'd never tasted better brownies, but I'd be darned if I'd ask for the recipe. Taking my time, I rounded up my purse, searched for my sandals, picked up another brownie and stood there wondering where the heck I thought I was going all by myself, just to spite Johnny.

I'd eaten very little for supper and was paying for it now with a ravenous appetite. Feeling a bit drowsy and light-headed, I decided to take a rest before facing the sidewalk mob.

I settled into the big armchair wedged into the corner facing a window. I enjoyed sitting here, watching birds and squirrels in the trees.

Maybe Johnny would change his mind and come home to me, where he belonged. I was his wife, darn it, and it wasn't right for him to go traipsing off with a draft dodger and a hippie chick, for lack of a better description.

If he'd come back to me, I'd tell him the truth—that

I detested living here and wanted to leave, yesterday if not sooner. We should go somewhere we could lead a normal life.

Somewhere like home.

I dozed off with half of another brownie in my hand. The murmur of voices awakened me and I lay there, trying to gather my faculties. I had no idea how much time had passed or even where I was, at first.

"No, baby, no lights."

The smooth, murmuring female voice sounded strange to me, but not the voice that responded.

"Lights…lights in my head."

Johnny? I'd never heard his voice so breathless and spacey. I wanted to jump up and find out what was going on but every muscle felt atrophied.

I heard shuffling feet, a few giggles… Lise and Johnny, scuffling in the dark. I licked my lips, closed my eyes tight and then opened them to the same over-powering blackness.

Do something, Frankie!

A crash, the creaking of bedsprings. They couldn't be in our bed!

Lise's murmuring voice broke through my thoughts. "What do you see, Johnny? What do you see?"

There was a long pause and heavy breathing, and then Johnny said, "God. I see God and the entire universe. Where am I…in heaven?"

"Give me a minute and you will be."

More noises that confused me—the rustle of fabric, the slide of a zipper, then a groan from Johnny.

"I'm flying…Frankie, baby…"

I couldn't stand it. Feeling sick to my stomach, I flailed around, trying to rise to my feet. Something doughy crushed in my hand. The brownie…my second or third? Or fourth? Delicious brownie.

Lise's murmurs curled my toes. "Never before, huh, Johnny? I knew it. You're a wannabe. You've just been along…for the ride. And now you're tripping on your own because that bitch you married pissed you off."

"Frankie. Beautiful Frankie. I see her…"

"You'll see lots of things, baby, better things than that uptight bitch."

Heavy breathing. Then Lise murmured, "You like that, dude? Hang on because now this trip is on, there's no getting home early."

He mumbled something but I couldn't make it out. On instinct, I stumbled toward the door, reached for the light switch, flipped it on.

There was a sharp gasp from the bed, and I turned to see Lise in her birthday suit astride an equally naked Johnny. His head was arched back and his wide-open eyes stared at something I would never see.

Nor did he see me, but Lise did. She straightened up on his body, rotating her hips, smiling.

"Well, well," she murmured. "This couldn't have happened any better if I planned it."

"You bitch," I said in a dull, low voice. I'd never said that word aloud before, not even about a dog. "You *did* plan it. Get away from him."

"Can't. Not now. Why don't you split and come back later."

I wavered, reached out to steady myself with a hand on a chair "I…I…"

She laughed, and her steady movements continued. "Enjoy the brownies?"

"The brownies?"

"You ate some, right?"

"Well…uh…"

"I made them special for you. Feel a little light-headed?"

"I…that's not—"

"Pot," she said. "I put pot in the batter. You're on your own trip and too damned dumb to know it."

"But…" My tongue tripped over the single word.

"You don't want to be here," she said flatly. "The things I plan to do for this cat are not things that you even know about. Get out."

In despair, I grabbed the doorknob, helpless to resist her. I didn't know where I was going but if I stayed here, I'd either die…or kill her.

I stumbled out into the dark hall, shaking and nauseated. I felt sick, unable to think. I turned left and plowed straight into one of the walls that provided niches for each apartment door.

Hands pressed flat against the wall, I slid to the floor and huddled in the corner. What was wrong with me? I should be in there throwing Lise out the second-floor window with Johnny right behind her.

Johnny. How could he do this to me—to us? Others pursued casual sex, many others including my father and brother. But not us. We were *married.* We were committed to each other for life, not just playing around like the rest of these people.

Destroyed, tears rolled down my cheeks, although I made not a sound. What was I going to do now? I couldn't go back in there and I couldn't spend the night here. Already the smells in the hall were getting to me: sweat, booze, mold and many other noxious odors I couldn't identify.

My fragmented thoughts skipped forward and backward. For this I broke with my family...left home...trusted him. He neither loved nor respected me....

Death slipped into my mind. Maybe—

A figure stepped up to the door, a dim shadow in the faint yellow light of the bare bulb down the hall. He reached for the doorknob, then apparently caught sight of me.

"Frankie?"

Ben-Boy, sounding as sober as a judge and disbelieving as well. "Is that you down there on the floor?"

I gulped hard and mumbled an almost incoherent yes.

"You up for company?"

I wanted to say, no, no, I'm not up for company and especially not from you. You should be keeping Lise busy and away from my husband.

But I didn't say a word and Ben-Boy sat down on the floor beside me, slipped a friendly and much-needed arm around my shoulder. "Is Lise inside?" he asked.

I burst into real tears and clung to him.

"Calm down, babe. It isn't the end of the world."

"It's the end of *my* world!" I snuffled back tears. "I don't know...what's wrong with me? I wanted to kill her...still do, but...just came out here, c-collapsed."

He rubbed his fingers against my shoulder. "You didn't eat any of her brownies, did you?"

"Maybe. S-some."

"Babe, those were pot brownies."

"That's what she said, but I d-didn't believe her. Actually, they were...quite good."

"I'll bet. Listen to me. Lise put weed in those brownies. She had every intention of bombing you to finally get her mitts on old Johnny."

I jerked away from his comforting arm, feeling dizzy from the effort. "You knew? She's *your* girlfriend."

"She's everybody's girlfriend. I got no rights to her. You know, flower children and all that crap. Share and share alike. Look, babe."

He twisted around as if trying to see my face. "Johnny's gonna be in tough shape for the next few days. She gave him a whole bunch of acid and he's not used to it."

"He sounded…strange. I knew…drugs." I gulped back a cry of disbelief.

"Yeah, but that's not his usual thing. She put the moves on him, you know? And he was upset because you didn't come with us. He's been under a bunch of shit, trying to keep you all sweet and pure in the middle of this scene."

"Then why did he b-bring me here?"

"He digs you, babe. You're all he talked about before he went back to get you—damn, he even married you. What was the point of that?"

"I wouldn't have come without it."

"Smart." He nodded his head wisely. "I don't know what he sees in you, uptight like you are. Here's what I want you to know—it's gonna take him two or three days at least to come down off this head trip. When he crashes, it won't be pretty. Right now he's floating but he's not used to dropping acid that way. Show some mercy, okay?"

"Not okay. I won't live with a…druggie. *I can't.*" I gritted my teeth, still feeling a little ill myself.

"Ah, give him a break. He's been bottled up all his life, one of the good guys. Everybody needs to bust loose once in a while. I feel sorry for the dude, even if he's got more money than God."

Something in his tone penetrated my addled brain. "I think you feel sorry for yourself, too. You sound kind of…" I searched for the word, couldn't find it.

"I am kind of," he agreed, his tone bleak. "I don't wanna go to Canada, Frankie."

I felt a lightening in my heart. "Then don't. Do your duty."

"You mean go to war? I don't want to do that, either."

"Because you don't believe in violence," I said, remembering all the comments I'd been hearing.

"Hell, no. I don't give a shit about violence. I don't believe in getting hurt. I don't believe in people shooting bullets at me. I don't believe in uniforms and taking orders."

"Oh." I hardly knew how to respond to that. Finally I said, "Then why don't you go home?"

"Home?" He sounded astounded at the thought. "I haven't been home for more than a year."

"Then it's time. Where is your home, Ben?"

"Denver. Lots of square establishment types in Denver."

"A mom and dad?"

"Yes. And a kid brother."

"Go home, Ben-Boy. Set an example for your brother. Find your answers there."

"Maybe…maybe I will."

He slouched down and cuddled me in his arms. Within a few minutes, his regular breathing turned into snores.

Ben would go home, but where would I go?

I COULDN'T SLEEP but Ben-Boy continued to snore. Sometime later, when dawn began to pierce the gloom, Lise wandered out of my room, yawning, carrying her clothing in her arms, weaving when she took a step. I swear, if I'd had a gun I'd have shot her dead.

Fortunately I didn't. I went inside the room, turned on the lights and pulled out my suitcase. I packed up a few things, crying so hard I could barely see. Johnny lay sleeping in our bed, naked as a jaybird, his arms flung wide. He didn't even know I was here.

Suitcase finally at the ready, I prepared to do something I dreaded—call home and eat crow. But first I went into our tiny bathroom and splashed cold water on my face, trying to calm down.

Red eyes and nose, a wrinkled forehead and an expression of total misery stared back at me from the cracked and yellowed mirror. This was my first—and last—home with Johnny Davis. I wanted to scream and howl, so sad that this is all that came from those schoolgirl fantasies I had about Johnny, but what good would that do?

I woke my mother up in the middle of the night. "Hi, honey," she said in a groggy voice. "I'm so glad to hear from you. Uh…is something wrong?"

I hesitated for a beat. "I…want to come home, Mother. Can I?"

I felt her sudden tension through the wire before she ever spoke a word. In the background, I heard Daddy ask, "What is it, Mary?"

"Nothing, Mike. I'll tell you later. Go back to sleep." To me she said, "What is it? What's happened?"

"I can't tell you on the phone. Can I come?"

"Of course you can come home. The sooner the

better. What has that boy done to you? If he hurt you, I swear I'll sic your brothers on him!"

Like a child, I let the tears flow once more. "I can't talk about that right now. I just want to get out of here."

"Do you need money for the plane?"

"N-no I've got enough." I licked dry lips. "Mom, thank you. After the way I left—"

"Baby girl, I was young once myself. I made my own mistakes and so does everyone else. I told you to come home anytime and I meant it. I'll be so glad to have you back. You'll have to fly into Kansas City. Let me know when to pick you up."

"I will."

"Frankie, honey, I love you. No matter what, I love you."

"I love you, too, Mom."

Damp-eyed, I hung up the receiver and turned around to find Johnny sitting unsteadily on the edge of the bed, his eyes still glazed and spacey. "Baby." He held out his arms, his smile wavering.

He was still high as a kite. Thank God Ben-Boy warned me.

I walked toward the bed, stopping out of his reach. "Johnny," I said in a wobbly voice, "I'm leaving you."

His brows rose in astonishment. "Leaving me! You love me and I love you. Come here and I'll show you."

What a beautiful boy, beautiful of body and a face now as innocent and open as a child's. He seemed to have not the foggiest idea that anything could have happened to upset me.

I filled him in with slashing words. "You came home smashed on acid, and you slept with Lise in *our* own bed." I clenched my hands, my nails cutting into my palms. Anger felt good, much better than misery.

"But…but you're the one I love. Come with me, angel, and we'll fly together. You don't know what sights there are to see—" He fell back on the bed, his eyes closing and his lips parting. "Fly away…the things you'll see…the colors and the— Come with me…"

"Goodbye, Johnny. I'm going home."

"Home. Home is here… I love you… I love you…"

God! And I grew up thinking *alcohol* was bad. Little did I know.

I dropped Frank Sinatra's silver dollar and my wedding ring on the bed and turned away.

MOTHER AND DADDY met me at the Kansas City airport and even he acted a little subdued. Mother looked awful, tired and drained and maybe even sick. Had I done that?

She covered a cough with her fist and slid her other arm around my waist. "We're glad you're home, Frankie," she said in a voice a little rougher around the edges than I remembered.

"Are you sick?" I asked in alarm.

"Just some kind of virus that's going around. Nothing to worry about."

Daddy took my suitcase and gave me a gruff, "Welcome home, kid," then led us out of the airport. I followed, feeling weary and downhearted.

My life wasn't supposed to end this way.

FOR A MONTH, I heard nothing from Johnny. In that time, I think I managed to catch Mother's virus because I wasn't feeling too hot myself. Food nauseated me and I felt all jumpy, nervous and anxious—Johnny's fault, no doubt.

Then, one morning at the breakfast table, Mother told me I was pregnant.

"No way," I said, looking down with distaste at the slice of toast on a saucer next to my coffee cup. "That would be the last straw."

Mom poured coffee into my cup. It looked as yucky as the toast and I pushed it away. "What makes you think that?"

"You just have that *look* about you. When I heard you throwing up in the bathroom yesterday, like you did the other time you were pregnant—"

"I must have caught that bug you had," I protested. Pregnant! How many more shocks could I take?

"You're married, honey. It's respectable for you to be pregnant. How many periods have you missed?"

"Maybe two…or three. But that's because I've been under a lot of pressure."

"It wasn't caused by pressure." She smiled. "To tell you the truth, I won't mind being a grandma. You're young, but you're strong and healthy, and you'll have a strong and healthy baby."

Our gazes met and I knew she was thinking about the baby I'd given away. A wave of agony cramped my stomach, and I laid my head on my arms, which were crossed on the tabletop.

Mother let me cry and when I looked up, she handed me a cold, wet washcloth. Obediently I pressed it against my eyes and struggled to collect myself.

"I'm divorcing him," I said. "You understand that, right?"

"I know that's what you said. But now with a baby on the way…"

I dropped the cloth and glared at her. "You don't know what he did to me! I could never take him back."

"You've been real tight-lipped about that. Was he unfaithful?"

Her direct question made me shudder. Despite my anger at Johnny, I didn't want to bad-mouth him to my mother or anyone else.

Nevertheless, she read my face. "Unfaithfulness is horrible," she said in a low voice.

The ice around my heart melted. We both knew this pain and I had treated her abominably, as if I were above such things.

"Mom," I whispered. "I'm sorry for what I said when I found out about Daddy. I didn't know what I was talking about. Now I do."

"I know you didn't mean it."

"But I won't react as you did. I couldn't just forget anything happened."

"Is that what you think?" She stared at me. "I never forgot and it never stopped hurting."

I covered her hand with mine. "I've got to get hold of myself and start acting like a grown-up. I can't lie around feeling sorry for myself."

"And Johnny?"

"He apparently got over me without much trouble. What could he possibly say now?"

"You're about to find out. Don't let your pride get in the way." She squeezed my hand. "He showed up on our doorstep this morning. He's sitting out back waiting to see you and says he won't leave until he does."

CHAPTER ELEVEN

JOHNNY HUNG AROUND for three days, much of it in my backyard or parked at the curb, and for three days, I stayed in my bedroom with a pillow pulled over my head. I couldn't see him. I just couldn't. If I did, there was no telling what he'd talk me into.

But I also couldn't live forever like a hermit. My first appointment with the doctor was Friday and I would not miss it. Maybe my mother was wrong.

Yeah, and maybe the sky wasn't blue.

A baby. My heart swelled with bitter gratitude at the thought—bitter because I'd given away my firstborn, gratitude that I'd have a chance to make up for that now. I would be the very best mother I could possibly be

The horrible thing, though, was that I couldn't give my baby a daddy who'd betrayed us both. My mother might be able to, but not me. I wouldn't do that to my child.

On the day of my appointment, as my mother and I left the house, I glanced around quickly. No Johnny.

Damn him! He'd already decided I wasn't worth the bother, I supposed. Maybe he'd gone back to Lise. It was a bitter pill to swallow, but the thought strengthened my resolve.

I walked into the doctor's office, half expecting to see him there waiting for me. Still no Johnny. He didn't even know about the baby, so why would he be here?

Mom didn't take a seat beside me in the waiting room. "I've got to run by the grocery store," she said. "I'll be back before you get finished here."

I nodded, feeling anxious that I'd have to do this all alone, then annoyed because a girl like me who was old enough to get pregnant—*twice*—should be old enough to carry through with it.

I shouldn't have worried. Dr. Payton had been our family doctor since before I was born and he was all patience and gentleness. By the time I walked out of the building to find my mother, I felt a deep glow of satisfaction with myself. I could do this.

My mother was nowhere in sight, but Johnny was, standing beside the convertible we'd driven to California, holding the door open, waiting for me to get inside.

I didn't want to. Why should I? I lifted my chin and glared at him.

He said my name with such grief and longing that I almost ran into his arms. Almost. I couldn't be pacified that easily.

"What are you doing here?" I asked coldly. "Were you following me?"

"Yes."

"You've got some nerve!"

"Always have. Get in the car…please. I have to talk to you."

"Why?" I wouldn't make it easy for him in any way. He'd put me through hell, and it was going to take a lot of work for him to make me even consider being with him again.

"Because…my draft number's come up. It's either Canada or Vietnam. You're still my wife, and I won't make that choice without you."

JOHNNY PARKED the convertible on that well-known bluff overlooking the creek and turned off the engine. I sat there in silence, feeling nauseous and weak as a kitten.

Vietnam. For some reason, I hadn't thought about Johnny going there.

After the longest time, he turned to me, his handsome face grim. Somehow he seemed like a completely different person. "I'm sorry," he said.

"For what?" I said, trying to remain cold and tight.

"For disappointing you, I guess is the best way to put it."

"You slept with Lise! God!" I curled my hands into impotent fists. "You did drugs."

He looked me right in the eye. "I swear, I don't remember what happened with Lise. I know you're right because Ben-Boy told me about it, but I don't remember."

"You don't *want* to remember."

"I suppose, but it isn't only that." He closed his eyes, as if trying to see the horrible scene. "I'd never taken acid before and it was a real bad trip. You were long gone before I came out of it and I had so many flashbacks—" He swallowed hard. "All I really know is that I threw away the thing I wanted most—you, you and me together."

"That's over and done with. You know I'm divorcing you I asked your mother to tell you." Just saying the words cut me to the quick.

He nodded, a fierce look in his eyes. "Dammit, I love you just as I always have. I don't want a divorce."

I spoke above the pounding of my heart. "Neither do I. But I won't stay with a man who cheats on me."

"Don't you believe in second chances? *I* made a mistake. I'll never ever do it again, I swear to you."

I froze at his words. I'd made a mistake far worse than his, now that I let that memory slide back into my mind. He'd been high on acid; I'd been stone-cold sober when I gave away our child.

"You don't make mistakes, Frankie," he said wryly. "You always know what you're doing."

That was a long way from true.

"It's over. I wish you well, but this is the end." My voice didn't sound nearly as firm as I'd have liked.

"In that case, I don't suppose it matters whether I head to Canada or to Vietnam."

I thought about that for a moment before answering. When I did speak, my words came slowly and painfully. "I don't want you to go to Vietnam, but even more, I don't want you to run off to Canada like a coward," I said. "A man does his duty for his country and the people he cares about."

I took a deep breath and straightened against the plush leather seat. "But I can't tell you what to do," I added. "I have no right."

"Don't you? You're pregnant with my baby."

My heart skipped a beat. "Who told you that?"

He shrugged. "Who do you think? Your mom told my mom. You may want to write me off, but I'll always be a part of my baby's life—my *son's* life."

A boy. He thought I would have a boy, and from the light in his eyes I saw how much that would mean to him. "I would never try to keep you from this child," I said. What a bind I was in now. "Will you take me home, please?"

"Sure. But first you might like to know that Ben-Boy decided not to go to Canada. He went home to his folks and they took him back. They talked about it and he's decided to go into the army."

"Good for him."

"And Lise—"

"I don't want to hear about Lise."

"Lise is dead. She OD'd a few days after you left."

As much as I hated Lise and had wished her dead, I felt terrible that she was.

"I don't want to hear any more," I said in a strangled voice. "Take me home. Then you can do whatever you want about the draft, as long as you leave me out of it."

"I can't, honey." He started the car. "Divorce me if you will, but we'll always be a couple—always. Some things can't be changed."

A couple of months later when I heard he'd joined the marine corps, I remembered his words.

Some things really *can't* be changed.

THE JOY OF Laura's birth brought bittersweet memories. Holding my baby girl close to my breast, I wept tears for that other child and prayed that his life was a good one.

Laura Diane Davis, the cutest and smartest baby in the universe, had the entire world wrapped around her little finger from day one. Every time I looked at her I grieved that Johnny wasn't here to see how perfectly wonderful she was. And my next thought would be *thank heaven he isn't.*

I wrote a dutiful letter to him, of course, telling him of Laura's arrival and including a picture. Mail took forever to get from here to there. I heard from him in mid-July, and his letter was full of longing to hold his child in his arms. As usual, he included no information about the war.

Back at home with my parents and my baby girl, I found myself strangely discontented. I wanted to live on my own, to take care of Laura and myself without my family constantly hovering. As much as I loved them, I needed space.

Still dissatisfied, I went back to work at Mother's café, taking Laura with me. Sitting in her baby seat on the counter near the cash register, she charmed the customers and was never without the attention of her mother and grandmother.

Everything would have been perfect if only… I fought to keep my thoughts from Johnny and the dangers that surrounded him. I had pushed ahead with the divorce, but still I was unable to bear hearing any bad news about what was going on in Vietnam. I avoided reading newspapers and watching TV news reports and hearing conversations about the war. What I didn't know couldn't hurt me.

Then letters from Johnny stopped coming, and because we were no longer married, I received no news. I lived on the edge during that time, each ring of the phone or knock on the door bringing alarm.

Weeks later, his mother called from Florida, where she'd taken a vacation home, to tell me he'd been wounded and was in Bethesda Naval Hospital in Washington, D.C. She said it kindly, but that didn't lessen the shock.

Without hesitation, without considering friends or family. I packed up my child, my bags and my courage to make the drive to Kansas City where I took a plane east.

I'd been on an airplane only once before but love versus fear was no real contest.

I STOOD OUTSIDE a curtained cubicle in the hospital ward, ten-month-old Laura in one arm, a diaper bag over my other shoulder. The tall marine serving as my guide gave me a sympathetic glance.

"Sgt. Davis is in there, ma'am."

"Thank you for bringing me." My breath came shallow and anxious as I stared at the curtain.

"Glad to help, ma'am." He started to turn away, then hesitated. "Sgt. Davis is a good marine, ma'am."

Tears welled in my eyes. "Thank you for saying that. I can imagine no higher praise."

He nodded and walked away, his back straight and proud. I took a step toward the curtain, reached out to touch it, afraid of what I might find. Slowly I pulled away the barrier and saw Johnny at last.

He lay on the hospital bed, asleep. My lips parted in amazement. He barely looked like the Johnny I knew. Thinner, gaunt cheeks, lines of strain on his face even in rest... A gauze bandage wound around his temple. Scratches and scrapes and bruises in various stages of healing dotted his face, and a cast covered his left arm from hand to armpit.

I stared at him until Laura grew impatient and tried to wiggle free. I could barely tear my attention away from him to tend to her. All the love I'd felt for this man—this man, no longer a boy—overwhelmed me. Unshed tears filled my throat with grief and relief.

Lowering the diaper bag to the floor, I stood Laura on her feet and held her impatient little hand in mine. She immediately tried to climb onto the bed. Hanging on to her, I leaned over to whisper, "I love you, Johnny Davis." I dropped a light kiss on his forehead. I hadn't intended to wake him but his blue eyes instantly opened.

"Frankie." He spoke in a raspy tone, as if unaccustomed to speaking. "You came."

"You knew I'd come. I'll always come when you need me." I felt the trail of tears on my cheek. "I brought someone with me."

"You're enough all by yourself."

"I think you'll change your mind when you meet Miss Laura Davis." I plucked her from the floor and deposited her on the bed. "Laura, meet your daddy."

He stared at her as if afraid to touch her. "She's beautiful," he whispered.

"Bald head and all?"

"She'll have her hair someday…won't she?"

He looked so alarmed that I laughed. "You don't know much about babies," I teased. "Of course she'll have hair. Just give her time."

"I will," he promised. "Will you put her up here where I can reach her with my good arm? I never had a baby before."

That remark burst the dam and now my tears flowed without restraint. While he played with his daughter, I pulled a chair next to the bed and put my hand on what I could reach—his thigh, rock hard beneath the sheet.

While they got acquainted, I put my head down on the bed and counted my blessings.

"Marry me, Frankie. The thought of you and the

baby kept me alive over there. All I wanted was to get back to you. Marry me again."

I looked into the face of the only man I'd ever loved and I wavered. Despite all my grieving over the death of my marriage, despite the sleepless nights, despite his betrayal. I wavered.

He looked so helpless lying there on a white-sheeted bed in a ward with other Vietnam victims.

I could barely imagine how it must feel to be pinned down by enemy fire, by men trying to kill you. It was easy enough for me to tell him to do his duty and go to war; much harder for him, and all the men who faced the violence of that unpopular war.

Laura struggled to escape my tight grip. I soothed her, patted her, and tried to find the answer to his question

"Let's not talk about that," I said at last. "Tell me how this happened."

He shook his head. "I don't think I'll ever be able to talk to you about that," he said. "I saw things...did things... I don't want to remember any of it. I did my duty as best I could. Now I just want to go home to my wife and my child and find out what it's like to be alive again."

"Johnny, we're divorced."

"You love me, Frankie, and God knows I love you. I've never stopped loving you. Being in that jungle hellhole only made me love and miss you more."

I loved him more, too, but how could I go back to him after he'd been unfaithful? The unfairness of life crushed down around me, but I would not cry—I wouldn't! Not anymore.

He arched his head back against the pillow. "You're

remembering," he said. "I see it in your face. You're remembering all the things that happened in the Haight."

"Not all the things, Johnny. Just one—you and Lise
in bed together, me stumbling around on a brownie
high I didn't even know I had."

"I'd give my right arm to wipe all that out."

I stared at him, aghast. He'd already given much of
his left arm. What did I want, more blood?

I reached out to stroke his cheek. "You never did
remember that night, did you?"

"No, but I know what happened. I haven't touched
acid or any drug since, not even pot. I didn't even want
morphine for my injuries. I knew back then it was time
to get us both out of the Haight but it was hard to break
away from that sense of freedom, the camaraderie I felt
with Ben-Boy and the others. I know I was unfair to
you, over and above what happened with Lise."

"I want to believe you."

"Then believe me. That wasn't me back there. It was
some drugged-out idiot. I take full responsibility for
what I did but I swear to you, I'll never be unfaithful
to you again. I've had a lot of time to think since I got
here, and I have everything all figured out for us."

"I'm speechless." To have him take charge this way
filled me with relief. I was tired of making all the decisions, never sure of myself, always longing for his cer-
tainty.

"You haven't even heard my plans yet. We'll live in
Fairweather, but I'll go to Chicago a time or two each
month to help Dad with the business. You and Laura can
come with me, at least until she's old enough for
school."

"But—"

"I'll build you a house all your own, Frankie, anyway you want it."

"Money—"

"Will never be a problem for us, I swear. I've already inherited a lot and there's more to come. But I don't want to turn into a bum because of that, you know? I want to do things that count."

Impressed, I asked, "What kind of things?"

"I want to help our little town. Does that sound stupid? I want to open an office and invest in Fairweather and help it survive and get better for us and our children."

"I'm overwhelmed." And I was.

"I have selfish motives," he said. "I'll love you and our children and we'll be together for the rest of our lives. We need a town that's up for that."

He reached out to me, and Laura giggled, grabbing for his fingers. It almost seemed as if she sensed this stranger's importance in her life.

He smiled. "A little girl needs her daddy," he said softly. "Marry me, honey."

I hesitated, trying to take in all he'd said. Then, from behind the fabric curtain surrounding his bed, came a plaintive call. "For God's sake, lady, marry the guy and let the rest of us get some rest!"

JOHNNY AND I married three weeks later, the day after he got out of the hospital. Our simple ceremony, performed by a navy chaplain, thrilled me. No Las Vegas glitz or glamour here. When Johnny pulled our original wedding rings out of his pocket, my heart skipped a beat. This was a far better start for a new marriage than the first time, I thought, as he slipped the ring on my finger. We're both older and wiser and *not* headed for Haight-Ashbury.

Over champagne and brunch, Johnny leaned forward and gently laid our Vegas silver dollar beside my plate. Laura, on my lap, leaned forward with the speed of light and grabbed the coin, thrusting it directly into her mouth.

"Hang on, sweetie!" Johnny extracted the coin from her grubby fist. "That's your mama's wedding gift, not yours."

I smiled at him and picked up the coin. "You kept it," I said. "I wasn't even sure you'd find it."

"It's our good-luck token," he said with a smile. "We'll need all we can get when we tell our folks that we've more or less eloped—again."

HE SURE GOT THAT RIGHT. Both his mother and mine were beside themselves at the news. Both fathers wisely ignored the uproar.

"You could have waited until you got back home, at least," my mother complained.

His mother, freshly returned from Florida, added, "Such haste is inappropriate. You are such a disappointment to me, John."

"Now, Ma—"

"We'll hold a reception for you, of course," my mother said, smoothing the waters. "We can do it here—"

"Not at all! We'll hold it in the garden at my place."

"Now, Dorothy, as the mother of the bride—"

We got out of there in a hurry. The only reception we really wanted was an opportunity to reconnect with our old school friends, and that was *not* what the mothers had in mind.

'It'll be okay," I assured Johnny. "It won't hurt us to make them happy this time. We did manage to avoid a big wedding extravaganza, thank heaven."

He took me in his arms. "You're quite a girl, Frankie. I thought all women wanted a big blowout with the long white dress and a dozen bridesmaids."

That made me laugh. "Maybe the first time, but we're on our second go-round, Johnny Davis."

"Second and last."

He kissed me, and all was right with my world.

IT TOOK A FULL YEAR to build our house. We'd chosen a spot near the edge of town, in an area lush with trees and grass and flowers. Planning and details for our home took up most of our days and what I had left I spent working at Reva's.

There was nothing ostentatious about our place and that's the way I wanted it—plenty of room for more children and room to welcome our friends and families. When everything was complete and we'd moved in, we threw a big barbecue and invited everyone we knew.

People spilled over the lawn, perched in the gazebo, wandered through the trees where we'd placed extra chairs and tables. Mother manned the grill, and Johnny oversaw the drinks.

The doors to the house stood open so those who wished could take a tour, which seemed a bit pushy to me but seemed to please everyone else.

"That's quite some house you got there," Brenda said, clinging to her husband Larry's arm. She'd done the very thing she shouldn't; got pregnant and roped Larry into a shotgun wedding. Their little boy was now three or four and the spitting image of his daddy.

Larry nodded to me and turned away. "I'm gonna go get me a beer," he told Brenda.

"Larry, you've already had—"

He ignored her and stomped away. She turned to me with a helpless expression.

"You girls were right," she said in low tones. "I never should have married Larry."

"I wish we hadn't been." I gave her a quick hug.

She shook her head. "Frankie—" She looked around to make sure no one was close enough to overhear. "I'm going back to school. I want to be a nurse."

"That's wonderful!"

"I start in September. Mom says she'll watch little Larry for me—" She glanced around suddenly and added, "Now where the heck has that kid got to?"

"He's over there hanging on his daddy's leg."

"That's a good place for him," she said dryly. "Is Joanie here yet?"

"I think I saw her go inside a few minutes ago."

"Thanks. I'll find her." Brenda smiled wanly. "And thank you for being a good friend," she said. "I hope someday I'll be as happy as you and Johnny are."

"I hope so, too." I watched her hurry away and turned to catch a glimpse of my handsome husband. Surrounded by friends, he glanced up, saw me and gave a little wave with the barbecue fork. He loved me, I loved him, and the second time around was wonderful.

CHAPTER TWELVE

LAURA WAS ALMOST FIVE when I became pregnant with our second child in 1972. I was pretty sure before I saw the doctor and he confirmed the news. We were thrilled.

I made straight for Johnny's office but he was out somewhere, his assistant, Tammy, told me. Rather than wait. I decided to pick Laura up at Mother's and tell her the news.

When I approached the house, I noticed Laura peering from a window. I waved, but she just dropped the curtain and disappeared.

She met me in the hall, her little face surprisingly grim.

"Where's Grandma?" I asked, bending to give her a hug.

"Grammy's sick." She pointed toward the living room.

Surprised, I led the way. Mother never got sick. Maybe she just had a headache or something, although even that would be strange.

I saw her reclining on the couch in the darkened room and hurried to her side. "Mom? What is it? What's wrong?"

"Oh, honey, nothing's wrong." Voice rusty, she gave a little cough and sat up.

I'd heard that cough before but this time it seemed somehow more frightening. "Mom, you're allowed to feel bad once in a while. That's what doctors are for. You don't have to be superwoman."

Another cough, which she tried but failed to hide. "I'm just a little tired," she said unevenly.

"You're also losing weight." I regarded her through narrowed eyes, trying to see her as a person with a potential problem, not my mother. "You get tired very easily lately, now that I think of it. Even walking to the mailbox leaves you breathless."

"Now, Frankie, don't go getting yourself all…"

She suddenly gasped for breath and couldn't finish her sentence.

I was really getting worried now. "Your face is swollen." Why had I never noticed this before? "I'm taking you to the doctor—now."

I expected her to argue, but she didn't. "Call your father," she said at last. "He'll take me."

"He knows you're not feeling well?"

She shrugged. "I suppose."

Laura said, her eyes as big as saucers, "Grandma's sick? Really?"

"Just a little," I assured her. "She needs the doctor to give her some medicine or something. Laura, will you call Grandpa for us and ask him to come home?"

Her head bobbed with her answer. "Yes, Mama."

"Do you remember his number at the store?" We'd been working on telephone numbers for some time now. "It's four—"

"I *know* that number, Mama." She gave me a scornful glance and marched across the room to the telephone table.

I sat beside Mother and patted her arm. "It will be all right," I assured her as if she were my child. "It's probably just laryngitis."

Only that's not what it turned out to be at all.

"LUNG CANCER," my father said, his head drooping and his voice only a ragged whisper. I had never seen him so distraught. "I can't believe it. Not your mom."

I couldn't believe it, either. I shot a panicky glance at Johnny, and he slipped an arm around my waist. I needed his support desperately.

"She'll get through this," I said, trying to prop up my father. "Scientists are doing wonderful things these days, finding new drugs and new ways to fight...this." I couldn't even get the awful word *cancer* out of my mouth.

Cancer killed people. All kinds of cancer, each more horrible than the other. Even the treatment could be horrendous for the patient.

I tried to shake such thoughts from my mind. "How long will they keep her in the hospital?"

"I don't know. There's a lot to do...tests and so forth." He looked up, his expression sad to see. "I don't think I can get along without her, Frankie."

Then why didn't you treat her better? I wanted to scream the words at him but his grief held me back. "You won't have to get along without her, not for long. When she comes home from the hospital we'll all help her recover from this."

Johnny added, "We'll do all we can, Mike. If she needs a nurse—"

The front screen door slammed and the rhythm of Laura's flying feet brought us all back to the present.

"Mama, can I go to play with Janet? Please?" She appeared around the corner and burst into the room with her final words.

Despite the gravity of what we were feeling, life was going on as usual. Tell a five-year-old that everything would be fine and chances are she'll believe you.

Daddy barely seemed to notice her. He stood up, his movements stiff. "I'm going back to the hospital," he said. "Visiting hours don't end until nine."

Laura smiled with blissful ignorance. "Tell Grammy I love her." She kissed her hand and blew the kiss to Grandpa. "Mama, Daddy, can I go to Janet's? Please?"

It was just another day at Grandma's house to her.

LATER THAT NIGHT, as Johnny and I prepared for bed, I gave him my news about the baby at last.

I must have sounded grim because he took me in his arms and patted my back. "Aren't you happy about this, sweetheart?"

"Of course I'm happy about the baby, but for it to come up now, with Mother so sick—"

"This will make her better." He kissed my forehead. "News of another baby is just what she needs."

"Will she be around when this baby comes? I couldn't stand it if she…if she…"

"Hey, let's use a little positive thinking here. If anything will cause her to fight this cancer she's got, it's the promise of a baby. We have to be strong, Frankie— hope for the best and leave it at that."

"You're right, but I'm not sure I can."

"I'll help you. I know how much your mother means to you but you won't let this put you down. You have to think of Laura, and your father and the new baby, too. You have to be strong, Frankie."

He gave me a gentle shake. "You can cry and holler all you want when it's just you and me in this bedroom, and I'll understand. Out there, beyond this door, you'll do what you have to do."

I drew a deep, shaky breath. "How would I get by without you, Johnny?"

"Poorly," he said with a grin. "Don't even think about it."

I WENT TO THE hospital the next day and there, holding Mother's hand, I told her she would be a grandmother again in a few months. Hearing the news, her face glowed with anticipation.

"That means I have to beat this cancer in time for the grand arrival," she said in her gravelly voice. "This is wonderful news, honey. Have you told your father yet?"

Mention of my father always made me withdraw a bit and this time was no different. But this wasn't about me, it was about her.

"Not yet," I said lightly. "I'll get around to it soon."

Her face darkened. "He loves you, Frankie, and the boys, too. Don't hold against him something that I long ago forgave."

"It's hard," I said truthfully. "I just don't understand why he did it or why you put up with it."

"You forgave Johnny, didn't you?"

That gave me pause, because it was true. Finally I said, "But that was only once. He'll never do it again."

"So we hope."

"Mother! He was high on LSD!" I'd never told her

that before and her eyes widened in shock. "He didn't even remember what he'd done until I was long gone. Even so, it took us some time to get past it."

"For *you* to get past it."

I raised my chin. "That's right. I have my pride, after all."

"You have too much pride, my girl. You're not perfect, even though you try to be. The rest of us have flaws and we learn to forgive and forget. Even when you forgive, you don't forget."

Her words cut deep, but I couldn't, wouldn't strike back, even though my lips trembled. "I'm doing the best I can," I said finally.

"Then do me another favor." She leaned toward me, a real effort. "Never tell your father what you know."

"Mom—"

"Promise me."

"But—"

"It would kill your father if he knew."

I doubted that. He was too brusque and too intimidating to take other people's feelings or opinions into account.

I wouldn't be able to talk her out of this, nor would I want to try. I saw such determination on her haggard face that it made me want to cry with hopelessness.

"All right," I said. "I promise I'll never tell him that I know what a two-timer he is."

My mother relaxed and closed her eyes. "Forgive and forget," she breathed. "It won't hurt you to forgive and forget, Frankie."

How HAD WE not noticed? When Mother came home from her hospital stay, she looked even more gaunt and sick than before. I quickly added *weak* to her list of symptoms—even sitting up in bed proved difficult for her.

Having her back home was a blessing, though, for her and for us. I wanted to stay and take care of her, but Johnny pointed out that somebody had to run Reva's. Our only other choices were to sell the café or close it down.

Neither of those last two possibilities appealed to Mother or to me. Laura in tow, I did what I'd been trained to do. I took over the café. Since I wasn't comfortable leaving Mother alone, Johnny hired a registered practical nurse to live with and care for Mother.

We put her in my old room. Although I had had a house of my own now for some time, it came as quite a shock to realize that room in my parents' house would never again be mine.

Fairweatherites pitched in to help, as longtime friends and neighbors do. As my pregnancy advanced, people would come forward to help at Reva's, often sending me home for a much-needed rest. I took their assistance with gratitude, praying that someday Mother would actually be able to take over again. I missed having her at the café with me.

A couple of weeks before my due date, baby Katy made an early appearance. I went into labor behind the counter at Reva's, having those early pains that make you wonder if you're truly having the baby or if it's a false alarm. Taking no chances, the waitress called Johnny, who whisked me away to the hospital where Miss Katherine Marianne Davis made her appearance at six pounds, six ounces.

On my way home four days later, Johnny took me

by to show off our bundle of joy to Mother. I nestled the blanketed baby in her arms and stepped back to admire the picture they made.

"What's her name?" Mother gave me a quick glance. "Nobody would tell me."

"They didn't know. She's Katherine…Marianne… Davis. Named for you, Mother—Mary Ann, with a little different spelling."

Tears leaped to her eyes. "What a sweet thing to do, Frankie."

"It was Johnny's idea," I admitted, "one of his *better* ideas."

Johnny shrugged off our praise, but I could see it touched him. His own mother was in Italy and had sent a telegram and a check, as had his father in Chicago. He'd tossed them aside with a shrug I knew he didn't mean. Their aloof attitude hurt him still.

Local folks responded to him, however. He'd followed his dream to make a positive contribution to this small town. He also conducted family business from the new office building he'd erected in the downtown area, flying to Chicago several times a month to confer with his father about the automobile dealerships.

In the meantime, he was a soft touch for anyone who needed help, money or otherwise. I stayed out of his business for the most part, since my hands were full with kids and Mother and café.

I'd gotten used to our family situation over the months, settling into a routine that I expected to carry on indefinitely. I knew the chemo made Mother even sicker, but it was for her own good, as I'd heard so much as a child. At least, I desperately hoped so.

Her nurse, Greta, seemed to be growing more and

more grim, but I put that down to personality. She was no barrel of laughs on her best day. Maybe she needed more time off. I'd mention it to her the next time.

The next time never came. I went in to see Mother the next afternoon, kissed her, took her hands in mine. She looked at me, smiled and closed her eyes.

My hair practically stood on end; it was as if I could feel her life force leaving her body and passing through my hands. Her color began to change and blue tinged her mouth—

I screamed. "Mother!" I shook her hands urgently. "Mother, wake up! Say something! Please—"

Greta charged through the door and practically threw me aside. Pressing her fingers to Mother's wrist, she stood perfectly frozen with concentration.

I held my breath. Greta sighed and laid the arm gently on the bed.

"She's gone."

"No! That's impossible. It isn't time!"

"Honey, nobody knows when it's time but the Lord. Your mama hung on for that baby and once the little angel came, she more or less gave up."

Hot tears scalded my cheeks, but I wasn't crying tears of sadness. "Will you go call Daddy? I'll stay here with her."

"You sure you're okay with that?"

"As okay as you can be when you've just l-lost your mother."

Greta nodded; I could see she really did understand. Slipping onto my trembling knees next to the bed, I lifted Mother's hand and pressed it against my burning cheek. I felt no movement, no hint of a pulse.

I had never seen anyone die before and even now, I

couldn't believe it had happened. I lifted my head and, praying this was some kind of terrible mistake, said a tentative, "Mother?"

There was no movement, no response, no nothing. My mother was dead. Fervently I thanked God we'd said the things we needed to say when we still had time. She knew I loved her and I knew she loved me. It had to be enough.

WITH JOHNNY'S SUPPORT, I made arrangements for Mother's funeral. Daddy was completely incapable of making any decisions whatsoever, and somebody had to do it.

Besides, I didn't want to even try going on as usual because everyone I saw offered their condolences and I could hardly bear it. I knew everyone was sorry, but I couldn't provide comfort to them. I hadn't dealt with the death myself. This whole thing seemed like some kind of miserable nightmare that would never go away.

Flowers practically overran the Leacock Funeral Home. The floral aroma, usually so pleasing, made me sick to my stomach. Dressed in black more because it fit my mood than for tradition, I hid behind large dark glasses and tried to hang on to my self control.

At the graveyard, I closed my eyes behind those glasses because I couldn't bear to see her casket lowered into the ground. Johnny's hand tight on my elbow helped, and so did the nearness of my three brothers. They stood with bowed heads, guilt written all over their faces because they hadn't understood the gravity of Mom's illness. When my father moved to drop a beautiful white rose upon the casket in the grave, I turned abruptly into Johnny's chest and hid my face.

He held me close and I stood there until the ceremony reached its conclusion. I remembered the day as dark and gray, although he told me later that the sun actually emerged just minutes after we arrived.

Many had joined the funeral procession to the cemetery and now they paraded past for a handshake or a hug, offering a murmured condolence, Joanie among them.

She hugged me tight and whispered in my ear. "Call me if you need me. It'll be hard, now that you're the woman of the family."

Would people, would family, expect me to take Mother's place? I could no more do that than I could fly to the moon. Mother was a rock and I was…

To my and Joanie's surprise, I let out a faint chuckle. Mother was a rock and I had trouble being a decent pebble

If I tried really hard, could I learn?

Present

TIME CRAWLED PAST and Frankie fought the depression that settled around her like a storm cloud. It seemed as if she'd never get to St. Louis no matter how she tried. She seemed to crawl from one traffic jam to the next, from one wrecked car to another.

Stop-and-go traffic was bad; stop-and-stay traffic was worse, and that's the kind Frankie got stuck in. Disgusted, she turned off the engine since she wasn't going anywhere anytime soon and the car was drinking gasoline.

Sitting there surrounded by cars and ice, she thought about Johnny and all they'd been through together, both the good and the bad. She wondered, not for the first time, why she was making this trip from hell.

She stopped answering her phone, unwilling to explain anything to anyone.

Not even to herself.

CHAPTER THIRTEEN

DADDY NEVER GOT over Mother's death. To spare him more pain, I sorted through Mother's things for him a few weeks later, boxing up her clothing for charity, sorting through papers and keepsakes. To my surprise, I took pleasure in handling the items she'd loved, holding soft fabrics to my cheek, running my fingers over jewelry and keepsakes. Happy memories flooded me, pushing away some of the grief of her passing.

One day, I found it—the letter I wrote to Johnny all those years ago. I held it in my hand and stared at it, turned it over and saw that Mother had told me the truth. She hadn't opened it.

I started to crumple the blue envelope and then stopped short. Somehow I couldn't destroy it when it had changed my life so. When I left that day, I tucked it into my purse.

As time passed, Daddy took to drinking and ignored his hardware business and friends who sought to comfort him. Fortunately, my older brother Jerry took on the responsibility of the store. It was generally accepted within the family that it would eventually be his, anyway, as the café was now mine.

I watched Dad's grief and tried to think of a way to help him. He wouldn't talk, not to me or my brothers or anyone else.

Even Johnny tried to get through to him with the same results. Time crept past and we all held our breath, waiting for the inevitable.

On the anniversary of Mother's death, Daddy wrapped his pickup truck around a tree. He lingered in a coma for almost a week and then slipped away from us without even opening his eyes.

Although he'd refused my attempts to connect with him, I found some comfort in his death because I'd never revealed what I knew about his "extracurricular" activities. What good would it have done when the past was past? Mother had been right and always had been.

Perhaps I was growing up at last.

Holding tight to Johnny's hand, I told my husband for the first time what Daddy had done, how Mother had reacted. Johnny listened while I unloaded the entire story and then, instead of agreeing or disagreeing with me, he asked a question.

"Why are you telling me this now instead of when it happened?"

Flustered, I realized I had no good answer. I said weakly, "I don't know. Maybe I didn't want you to realize what a jerk my father was while he was still around."

"Or maybe you still loved him to the bitter end. And now I think you want me to realize that you'd never put up with a philanderer like your mom did."

"You're no philanderer," I said indignantly. "I've finally put your…transgression…behind me."

"Really."

He didn't believe me. "I have."

Johnny sighed. "I'll take your word for it. But about your father—I knew what he was doing. So did your brothers."

I stared at him in shock and surprise. "How on earth—"

He shrugged. "It seemed obvious to me, and then Jeff mentioned it. I think he needed to get it off his chest. I stayed out of it, though. Never stick your nose into somebody else's marriage."

IT TOOK A WHILE for life to settle down for us, with the deaths of both my parents to deal with. I found comfort in our girls, who grew like little weeds. Johnny was our rock, a great father to them and husband to me.

He kept a tight grip on his business affairs, from what I could tell, and I handled Reva's as Mother had taught me to do. Johnny and I went to Chicago frequently, girls in tow unless they were in school. In that case, they stayed with Jerry, and his wife, Mindy, who had no children of their own and had longed for them. Mindy had become my right-hand woman at the café, as well, and took over when I was gone.

Marriage to my favorite guy carried with it some obligations I would just as soon have skipped. Such as the present one.

"Do I really have to go?" I asked for the sixth or seventh time.

Johnny paused in the act of fastening his tie and grinned at me. He looked perfectly at home in this luxurious Chicago hotel suite while I always felt like a little match girl who'd wandered in by mistake. Still, I'd rather stay here than in the family mansion where he'd grown up. His father was, to put it kindly, a gloomy presence.

"You promised," he, the soul of patience, reminded me. "Lew and Gloria are expecting us."

"Along with all the hoi polloi in their fancy Lake Avenue apartment," I grumbled. "I never really liked them all that much in the first place."

He took no offense. "There'll be plenty of other people for you to talk to."

"I suppose but…but I miss the kids." Maybe whining would work.

"They don't miss us," he said, "not when they're staying with Jerry and Mindy."

"It's too bad your mom was out of town again, though. She'd have enjoyed keeping the kids for us."

His mother had remarried only days ago and was on a honeymoon cruise with her new husband. We'd come to Chicago—her new husband's hometown—for the ceremony and stayed on for Gloria's party.

"Your mother really likes Gloria," I said in a neutral tone, considering my defects in the mirror. She likes her more than me, but I didn't add that.

"Mom's known Glo for years." He came up behind me and put his arms around my waist, his hands gliding over the silky fabric of my emerald-green dress. "She grew up right next door to us, before we moved to Missouri and I found you."

He nuzzled my neck and I shivered. He still had the power to affect me with the slightest touch, and no doubt always would.

"Do you ever regret that?" The words stemmed from my lack of self-confidence when out of my own baili-wick.

"Moving to Missouri or finding you?"

"Don't tease. I mean both. Your life would have been completely different if you'd stayed here."

"Yeah, I'd be a displaced hippie in some gutter in

Canada." He turned me around in his arms. "No, thanks. I'm happy where I am."

His kiss warmed my lips and I clung to him, feeling reassured about Gloria. I just didn't like the way she acted around him, although Lew, Gloria's husband, didn't seem to notice. Was I just being a jealous fool?

No, not jealous, cautious. If anyone made a fool out of me, I wanted to be the first to know, not the last.

With a start, I realized Johnny was backing me toward the bed.

"We'll be late," I protested, not too strongly.

"So what? You don't even want to go."

"Yes, but—"

"No buts," he said, lowering me to the bed, ignoring the fact that I was all fixed up and ready to go. And not at all unhappy with this change of events.

GLORIA LEANED BACK in her lounge chair, the beauty of nighttime Chicago glittering behind her. She looked lazily at ease here toward the end of her cocktail party, as well she should. With so much help, all she had to do was smile and enjoy herself.

"I hope you had a nice time tonight," she said to me. "I know that big handsome husband of yours did. He's such a star in these social situations."

"I had a lovely time," I said primly. "I met a number of really interesting people."

"They were quite taken with you, too." She sipped daintily at her martini. "Darling Johnny is so good with strangers."

"He's good with everyone," I corrected, glancing at Johnny standing at the railing next to Gloria's husband. He must be enjoying the view, which was glorious.

"He tells me you're all excited about the bicentennial coming up," she said in the same languid tone.

"Well," I said, "yes. My Brownie troop will be marching in the parade and there will be a big community picnic following. I always help out with the food and Johnny helps with the—"

"Brownies!" Her voice held such astonishment at an everyday thing.

"I'm the leader of Laura's troop," I said. "Katy's too young so she'll have to wait to be a Girl Scout."

Johnny turned from the railing. "And a darn good leader Frankie is," he defended me. "Wait until you see those girls march!"

That made everyone laugh. "Of course," I said, "my husband, the former marine, taught them how."

He nodded modestly.

Gloria shook her blond head in disbelief. "Johnny, I never imagined you'd ever be an ex-marine or that—"

"Not ex," he interrupted. "There are no ex-marines, there are only former marines."

"I stand corrected. But I repeat, I can't imagine you playing drill man—"

"Drill instructor."

"—to a bunch of kids."

His grin widened, the grin that could charm birds out of trees. "Frankie did the hard work, I just got the fun. You know what else? All the girls wear costumes from designs from 1776, long dresses and aprons and puffy white hats. Frankie and the moms made them and they also—"

I had to stop this recitation before we bored our hosts into a coma. "Please, honey. We're going to have a great celebration for our country's birthday, that's all." I gave Gloria and her husband a bright smile. "Do you have any plans for the Fourth?"

Gloria picked up a wine bottle and gave it a shake, testing for contents. "We're going to the Riviera to get away from all this sentimental nonsense," she said. "To each his own."

Life without children certainly was different, but still, I felt sorry for her. Maybe she wouldn't be so self-involved if she had kids.

On second thought, I'd pity the poor child who had Gloria for a mom.

She rose and flipped back her Farrah Fawcett hair. "Johnny, will you help me choose another bottle of wine? It seems we're all out here." She hoisted the bottle.

"Sure."

That old uneasy feeling swept over me again. "Let *me* help you." Which was ridiculous, since I knew nothing about wine.

"I've got it, honey." Johnny followed our hostess toward the opening in the glass wall leading to the interior. "We'll be right back."

Lew clapped a hand on my shoulder, halting any possibility of my joining them. "And in the meantime, I'll mix up one of my famous Long Island iced teas for the lady, here."

"I don't think I want anything else after the wine," I objected, watching my husband trail Gloria's swinging hips into the luxurious white living room that must never have known a child. The bright colors of her long gown blazed against the bland setting.

"Now just wait until you taste this. You'll love it. It's my own secret recipe. It's got—"

"Excuse me." I didn't care what it had, I just cared about what was going on in the kitchen. "The rest-room is…?"

"Through the living room, turn left. And while you're gone, I'll just mix up a little ambrosia for your return."

I hurried into the living room and turned right. Just outside the kitchen doors I heard voices and stopped short.

Frozen to the spot, Gloria's words echoed in my ears.

"You can't *possibly* love that little hillbilly, Johnny. She's nice enough in a backwoods way, but she'll never satisfy you…like I can."

"Back off, Gloria. You don't know what you're talking about."

"Oh, but I do. I've known you all my life. I know what you want, what you need," she purred.

I could imagine her hands reaching up to stroke his face. I curled *my* hands into fists, fists that would hurt me as much as the person I slugged, so I'd been told.

I was more than ready to take that chance.

Why was I standing here, waiting for Johnny to speak? I might not like what I heard. Why didn't I just burst in on them and—

"Frankie? Where are you, hon?"

Lew's voice jolted me out of my frozen state with a start. I turned quickly and rushed back into the elegant and overdone living room.

I said a shaky "I'm here."

Lew came toward me, smiling, holding out a tall glass with a drink of a ghastly color inside. "I mixed you up one of my specials. I know you said you didn't want to get into mixed drinks after the wine earlier, but maybe you'll take just a little sip and tell me what you think."

I couldn't get that tall, cool drink into my hand fast enough. "Bottoms up," I said, and lifted it to my lips.

I'D NEVER BEEN drunk before in my life but now I *was*. After returning to our hotel by cab, Johnny almost carried me to the elevator and up to our room.

Neither of us said a word until we were safely inside. Once he'd deposited me on my feet, I collapsed onto the sofa.

He returned shortly with a glass of water and a couple of aspirin.

"Take them," he said, offering them to me.

"I don't have a headache," I muttered, shoving his hand away.

"You will. Trust me."

I took the pills and popped them in my mouth, then drank the entire glass of water before slumping back again. I knew I should tell him I was sorry, but after two of Lew's liquid masterpieces, was I *really* sorry?

Johnny regarded me for a few moments, his face sliding in and out of focus. He reached out to smooth my hair away from my forehead gently.

"What happened, honey? You were doing fine and then all of a sudden you almost fell off the couch. I know you had one of Lew's drinks, but that shouldn't knock you off your feet this way."

"Two." I held up what I thought were two fingers, although it might have been considerably more. I withdrew one, looked again and shrugged. "Some," I said.

"You'll be sick tomorrow," Johnny predicted, sitting beside me. He didn't sound angry, not even annoyed. "I guess I didn't know exactly how much you dreaded the party."

"It wasn't just that." My voice sounded funny, mushy around the edges. I turned to him suddenly and grabbed him by the lapels. At least I aimed for the lapels and finally got there.

"Do you love me?" I asked the question with complete sincerity. This certainly seemed the time for it.

"Babe, you're more drunk than I thought." He drew me into his arms until my cheek rested on his shoulder. "I love you more every day. You're my girl and will be until the last breath I take."

"Do you mean it?"

"Frankie!" He gave me a gentle shake. "What's got into your head now?"

"Gloria, I guess." I nuzzled closer, hoping he wouldn't put me away for my insecurity. "She lived next door to you. She thinks she knows you best." *She wants you*.

"Yeah, and she also wants Paul Newman and Robert Redford."

Had I said that last part aloud? I groaned.

"Honey," Johnny said, lifting me onto his lap, "I love you. Surely you know that by now."

"Yes, but once a long time ago—" I'd tell him now, I thought woozily. I'd tell him about that first baby now—

"Don't go back to Lise." He'd thought I was still dredging *that* up. He shifted me until he could look in my eyes. "You know how you feel right this minute?"

I answered that with a moan.

He nodded. "That's how I felt then, only a thousand

times worse. I don't even *remember* it, for chris'sakes. Will you ever be able to let it go?"

"I…I wasn't talking about… I wasn't—"

"Let it go. Let it go, baby. You told me you would—that you had. I love you and you love me. That's enough, isn't it?"

"That's enough." I echoed his words, confused by the turn of the conversation. What was the matter with me? Now was not the time for my confession.

Johnny lifted me off his lap and rose, then bent down to pick me up again.

"I know just what you need."

I closed my eyes and nestled against him. "You do?"

"Leave it to me."

He carried me to bed, I supposed. When he put me down onto my feet on the tiled floor in the bathroom, I wavered. There was a moment's quiet and some movement, then cold water plummeted down on me. I screamed and clawed at his hand, trying to get away. Maybe it would help if I opened my eyes.

His smiling face came into semi-focus, as did the shower stall. "Sorry, but you'll feel better once this is over."

"So will *you,* my love."

I gave him such a yank that he stumbled forward, tripped over the edge of the shower stall and fell inside—directly into the stream of icy water with me. He fought his way to his feet and we stood there, clinging to each other and ignoring the water pounding against us. Johnny started to laugh and I joined in, my head clearing a bit.

"I love you," he said against my chilly lips, and I repeated the words back to him.

Shoving aside the shower curtain, he climbed out and turned to pick up my shivering form in his arms. Water streamed off us, flooding the floor.

"Let's go to bed," he said.

"Good idea."

A good idea that got better and better.

Present

FRANKIE STOPPED for lunch that afternoon, needing rest more than she needed food. The café she chose reminded her of Reva's. She ordered the meat-loaf special and pulled out her cell phone.

"Everything okay at Reva's?" she asked Lynda.

"Fine and dandy. Where are you?"

Frankie sighed. "God only knows. The visibility is crappy and there have been so many delays that I'm not sure where I actually am. I'm okay, though. I just don't want you to worry."

"That's tough, but if anyone can get through, you can," Lynda predicted. "We'll be cheering you on, girl."

"Thanks. Talk to you later." Frankie clicked off the phone and sighed. Now she had to make good.

CHAPTER FOURTEEN

THE BICENTENNIAL PARADE in Fairweather went off flawlessly, along with everything else planned to celebrate the two-hundredth birthday of the country.

Red crepe paper decorated fireplugs, ribbons and bows festooned the bandstand and my troop received the "best marching group in the parade" blue ribbon. Johnny led the cheers while the girls went up to accept their honor.

After surviving that, life returned to normal. Mostly.

I chided myself every day for dwelling on what I'd overheard in Gloria's apartment. Johnny would never betray me, I knew he wouldn't. I reminded myself of this constantly, but still…

The man attracted beautiful and not-so-beautiful women the way ice cream drew kids. Why would such a man love me with the commitment I demanded? It just didn't make sense somehow.

Then one day, Lew called and asked Johnny to join him in California for a golf tournament in late May. "Frankie's invited, too, of course, but Gloria won't be here. She's going to a spa in Nevada."

"I'll talk to Frankie and let you know," Johnny said. Hanging up, he turned to me and relayed the offer.

"Since you're no fan of Gloria anyway, maybe you'd like to come along, since she won't be there," he said.

"You could shop, lie on the beach, do whatever pleased you."

"It does sound interesting," I admitted. "When is this going to happen?"

"Last week of May."

"Oh, Johnny, I can't go then. That's the last week of school. I always help out with the end-of-year parties and such. Plus, the girls would be so disappointed if at least one of us isn't there."

He looked disappointed himself. "Maybe I shouldn't go, either."

"It's up to you, but I don't think it's important that both of us be there. You could talk to the girls and see how they feel."

"Good idea. At the moment, I'm not sure how long I'll be in California if I decide to go. If I do, maybe you could come out for the last few days."

I shrugged. "We'll see how it works out," I said. "You never know…"

LAURA AND KATY weren't too happy their daddy wouldn't be around until he mentioned a "reward" for their patience.

"Disneyland!" Katy danced around the room, her dark curls flying. "In the summer?"

"That's right. Sound good to you, Laura?"

She laughed, all grown up at nine years old. "If Mom's gonna be here, it's okay if you go," she said. "You didn't have to bribe us, but now it's too late to take it back!"

And that solved Johnny's dilemma.

I SAW HIM OFF the last week of May and turned my attention to school affairs. We talked each night; he was enjoying himself and kept encouraging me to join him. He especially wanted me to come when his stay was prolonged by his father, who wanted him to check out several local Ford dealerships and consider expanding the business.

"I'm staying at Lew's condo in La Jolla," he said, trying to tempt me. "It's right above the beach and the view is fabulous. Lew will be leaving tomorrow to meet Gloria in New York, but he's invited me, or us, to stay here as long as we want."

"It does sound good," I admitted. "Let me see what I can arrange."

When I called him back to tell him I'd be in the next day, he was out. Rather than call again, I thought it would be a nice surprise if I just arrived, ready to enjoy some time alone. The kids were with Jerry and Mindy, and I drove to Kansas City to catch my flight.

I arrived after dark, and collected my luggage and grabbed a cab.

I'd been to San Diego before with Johnny and I really loved the town. This was the first place where I'd ever seen palm trees or a beach. Even the people here looked different, all tanned and supple and adventurous. They made me feel like a real pale face.

Smiling in anticipation once I arrived at the condo, I punched the doorbell and waited patiently. Nobody answered, and I wondered briefly if Johnny was out. I rang again just in case he was sleeping. The door opened and my smile disappeared. There stood Gloria Hitner, her hair mussed and a raincoat clutched tightly around her. She looked as startled as I was.

We stared at each other. "What are *you* doing here?" I demanded. "I thought you were in New York."

"What are *you* doing here? I thought you were in Missouri and *staying* there," she countered.

"Is Johnny here?"

"What do you think?" she said, and pulled the raincoat open. Beneath it, she wore nothing. She left the coat wide-open just long enough for me to realize that she was just a tad heavy through the hips.

I took a protective step backward, unsure of what I should do next. She solved that problem.

"Johnny?" she sang out. "There's someone here to see you, darling."

"He's not your darling," I said, fuming.

That's when my husband walked into view, also clutching a robe around him, a towel draped around his neck. His wet hair glimmered and light reflected off his damp face.

He stopped short, his glance flicking between his wife and Gloria. "What the hell—"

"Surprise!" I threw my arms out, my tone sarcastic.

"Frankie! You didn't tell me you were coming."

"I have to tell you so you can be prepared?" I felt my temper rising. "Is this what goes on when you take your so-called business trips?"

"What are you talking about?"

"It's too late. She already flashed me."

"Flashed you?"

"She's naked, as you very well know. Johnny, you promised!"

"You're kidding." He turned to Gloria. "You're naked under that thing?"

She gave a "what can I tell you" shrug.

"Tell her the truth!" he roared. "Tell Frankie that—"

"She already knows that I've always had the hots for

you. I'd never pass up a chance this good." She turned toward me. "And it was worth it. I'd do it again in a heartbeat…and so would he."

That did it. I threw my suitcase at Johnny and screamed, "You know how I feel about this! We're finished!"

The suitcase hit him right in the gut and he grunted, the breath knocked out of him.

"Calm down," he begged. "This is all a misunderstanding. I can explain—"

"I'd have to be blind and stupid to believe anything that comes out of your mouth. This is the end. It's over and done with—period. And this time, I mean it!"

I turned and marched away, my back straight and jaw tight. How had I known this day would come? Now that it had, what made me think I could survive it?

JOHNNY RETURNED HOME a day after me to find his belongings neatly packed in boxes and stacked by the front door. He stood in the middle of the living room, looking completely dumbfounded.

"What the hell is going on here?" He dropped his suitcases on the floor. "Gloria's a bitch, but hell! That's not enough to throw a man out of his house."

Keep your cool, I cautioned myself.

"I'm divorcing you," I said in a voice that should have been calm and collected, which it clearly wasn't. "You promised you'd never cheat on me again and you *have.*"

"The hell I have!"

"I saw it with my own eyes and heard it with my own ears."

He shook his head, hard and fast. "No, you didn't. You saw a setup. Gloria made it clear what she wanted, but I told her to leave. When she refused, I decided to go home. I'd just started packing when you arrived."

"Don't lie to me, Johnny. It only makes it worse." I turned my back on him. "You've slept with Gloria and I can't get past that. Not ever."

"You really believe that's what happened?"

The incredulity in his voice cut me to the quick, and I turned to face him. "Why wouldn't I believe it? It's not the first time."

He grimaced. "In spite of the years we've been together, in spite of everything we've shared, you're throwing me out? Haven't I proved that I love you? I told you I'd never repeat what happened in San Francisco, and I haven't."

I couldn't help it; tears dribbled down my cheeks. "I won't let any man humiliate me the way you have. Go. Leave me alone. My mother could overlook infidelity but I can't, especially when it's right in front of my eyes."

He took a rasping breath and picked up his suitcases, his face set in grim lines. "You're wrong about me, Frankie, dead wrong, as usual. I'm getting damned tired of this. I didn't sleep with Gloria and never wanted to. But if your mind is made up, I don't suppose you'd be swayed by reason."

He walked out and slammed the door.

That night I told Katy and Laura that Daddy wouldn't be coming back anytime soon, but that he loved them dearly. Their faces fell and then I did a despicable thing.

I said, "I know you're disappointed but…we're still going to Disneyland!"

And that's what we did.

MAYBE I SHOULD have thought about the humiliation of a second divorce from the same man before I got on my high horse. Everybody in town knew my business, of course. Friends made jokes, acquaintances cast pitying glances. I kept my chin up but it wasn't easy.

Nor was being a divorcée. The first invitation I got for a date rocked me back on my heels. "I can't go out with you." I exclaimed. "I'm a—" What? Married woman? I wasn't anymore. "—formerly married woman."

"Heck, Frankie, I know that," he said. "I don't hold it against you. We all make mistakes."

Unfortunately, Joanie heard this exchange over the cash register at Reva's. "Why didn't you go out with him?" she asked once he'd finally taken no for an answer. "You deserve a little fun."

"After you've had champagne, are you willing to settle for beer? I may not be married but I still have my standards."

She rolled her eyes at that. "Yeah, I know they're high. You're a hard woman to please, girl."

And so I was; no matter who asked me out, I kept refusing. Johnny returned to town frequently to visit the girls and they spent vacations and much of the summer with him. He treated me with complete indifference. which I returned, although I didn't feel it. I couldn't bear to think I might have made a mistake, but at the same time, I couldn't bring myself to consider another man, another relationship.

It took three years for me to realize that had to change. I swore I'd accept the next offer that came my way.

That would be Harold Bower, whom I'd known my entire life. He was really cool about it.

"Wanna go to the movies?" he asked without pre-amble.

All his invitation lacked was a "wink-wink."

"Harold," I said, "you've got yourself a date."

I was more nervous waiting for him to pick me up than I'd ever been before. I didn't want to go on a date. I didn't know how to act on a date. I knew I'd make a fool of myself.

"What's playing?" I asked as we motored toward Fairweather's only movie theater.

"I dunno. I think it's something about boxing."

I repressed a groan. Boxing? That wasn't even at the bottom of my list of favorite film topics.

I shouldn't have been so quick to jump to conclusions. The movie was *Kramer vs. Kramer* and it wasn't about boxing, it was about divorce and custody of a little boy, and it almost killed me. I was sobbing by the halfway point and never stopped. Harold shifted in the seat beside me and kept giving me alarmed looks but I couldn't help myself.

He bought me popcorn; I couldn't eat it and neither could he with my salty tears soaking it. When Meryl Streep won the court case, but then gave the boy back to his father, I practically howled in grief.

We walked out of the theater, me wet-faced and Harold shell-shocked and staying as far away from me as he reasonably could. I wiped off my face with a napkin from the concession counter and gave my escort an embarrassed glance.

"I'm sorry," I sniffled. "It was just so…sad."

"I thought it was kinda boring," he said.

"Oh, no! It broke my heart when they didn't g-get back together."

"I get it," he said. "You have been around the block a couple of times with old Johnny, haven't you?"

"My reasons for leaving were much better than the woman's in the movie," I said with all the dignity I could muster, but I was the custodial parent and Johnny had not objected. We never argued about the children because we accepted each other's rights, but what if he'd changed his mind?

I hoped if he ever saw this movie he'd discard any such notion, since the mother won custody even though she shouldn't have.

Back at the house Johnny had built me, Harold walked to the door and turned to me. "Well…"

He thought he could kiss me? Not in this lifetime! I grabbed his hand and pumped it up and down. "Thanks for the movie, Harold," I said quickly. "I had a wonderful time. Thanks. Thanks again."

Once inside, I peeked out the window. Harold still stood there in the glow of the porch light, and I'd have sworn that what he mostly looked was relieved.

IT'S FUNNY THE WAY time passes. It seems to creep by but all of a sudden you realize years have passed, you're older, your children are older and you don't really remember how it happened.

My girls were growing up nicely if I did say so myself. Katy, the baby at eleven, was a lively little tomboy who loved nothing more than duking it out with the boys. I drew the line at her playing football after one of her front teeth got chipped, but she liked baseball better anyway, she informed me.

Teenaged, Laura had budded into a young woman of grace and beauty. Like her sister, she was athletic; like her father, she was brilliant; and like me, she could be touchy from time to time.

Like now, when I discovered her crying in her closet and had the temerity to ask her why.

"I'm not crying," she sniffled, swallowing back tears. "I…I got something in my eye."

"Honey," I said, "I didn't just fall off a turnip truck. Sit down here on your bed and tell me what's going on."

She sat beside me, her head hanging. She said nothing.

I put an arm around her. Somebody had probably hurt her feelings, I thought, remembering my own sixteenth year with its ups and downs. "I'm your mother," I said gently. "You can tell me anything."

"There's nothing to tell," she said in a tight little voice. "I hate my sister, I'm failing half my classes and…I'm pregnant. Other than that, life's a bowl of cherries."

"Oh, Laura!" I folded her into my arms, feeling like a mother first and shocked second. "How did this happen?"

"The usual way, I suppose."

"Laura! You know what I want to hear. Who's the boy?"

"It's Mitch," she said miserably. "You know, the basketball player? You remember the night we went out and his car broke down?"

"Yes."

"Well, it didn't."

"Oh, honey…"

"Try to understand, Mother!" She turned her beseeching eyes on me. "I didn't want you to know because I knew you wouldn't understand. I know this doesn't live up to your standards but—"

"Laura Davis, don't give me that. You don't know what you're talking about." If only I could tell her, show her that it would come out all right. But I couldn't. I'd kept my own past a secret for so long that I couldn't even conceive what kind of damage its revelation might create.

She looked at me a bit sullenly, her lower lip thrust out. "I don't want Daddy to know," she said. "He doesn't need to know. We can handle this ourselves."

"Handle it how, pray tell?"

She groaned. "I don't know. I'm so confused."

"It's all right, Laura. We'll figure out something," I tried to assure her. "But your father must be part of it."

"Please don't tell him. Please. The two of you can barely talk to each other anymore. I don't want him mad at me, Mom. Please."

I held her hands in my own. "You underestimate your father, Laura. He'll understand."

She pulled away from me. "Will everybody else understand? This will be all over town. I won't be able to walk down the street without hearing the gossip."

I couldn't argue with that. "At this point, no one will know except you, me and your father."

"What about the brat?"

"Please don't call her that. Let's leave her out of the loop," I said dryly. "At least for now. We have a lot to think about and a lot of decisions to make. But first, I have to tell your father." I hesitated. "Unless you'd prefer to do it yourself."

She shuddered. "You do it. Please."

I nodded. "Okay." I patted her shoulder and rose. "Listen," I said to her, "I want you to relax and calm down. You're not in this alone anymore. Your father and I will be here for you, now and always."

Tears streaked down her cheeks. "Thank you, Mom." She rose and gave me a hug. "Thank you."

I watched her collapse on the bed and pull the bed-spread over her legs. I wasn't sure I deserved a thank-you but I was happy to hear it.

AFTER LEAVING Laura alone, my next decision was figuring out whether to call Johnny or just show up at his door in Chicago. Laura was right when she said we didn't speak that often and when we did, it wasn't always friendly.

This was different, though.

I'll call first, I decided. This was for Laura and I would make it work.

Present

NIGHTTIME. It was dark, cold and windy. Frankie fought exhaustion as long as she could and then gave in. Pulling into a motel parking lot, she hauled out her suitcase and made her way to the door through slashing frozen rain.

"We're full up," the woman behind the desk said re-gretfully. Frankie slumped at the words and the woman added, "You look done in."

She hesitated and Frankie prayed for a solution to the problem.

"Listen, I'll let you take the couch in the office. It's not the most comfortable thing in the world to sleep on, but at least you'll be warm. Old man Reeves wouldn't like it, but he's not here, right? In weather like this, you gotta help each other out."

"You're my fairy godmother. Lead me to that couch."

Frankie awakened stiff and still tired the next morning. Regardless, she knew she felt better than if she'd spent the night freezing in the car or looking for another motel. A quick cup of coffee and she'd be off again.

How much more of this could she take for a man who'd already decided that enough was enough?

CHAPTER FIFTEEN

I'D STARTED AVOIDING Johnny on his trips to Fair-weather over the seven years of our divorce. The more I saw him, the more I longed for him, no matter what had happened between us. Perhaps I was growing up at last. Or perhaps my standards were looking a little stupid by now.

He'd sold the family's Chicago home after the death of his father and established himself in a town house overlooking Lake Michigan. The girls loved it here, and I could understand why they'd be impressed by all the elegant touches even before I got to his door.

I steeled myself and knocked. Johnny opened the door and looked at me with caution. "What's going on, Frankie? Must be serious to bring you here." He said it carefully, as if he expected bad news.

He certainly had every right to be guarded, which didn't make me any more eager to drop my bombshell. It was not fun telling your ex that you're a lousy mother.

Especially when your ex looked this good. At thirty-seven, the same age as I was, he was still knock-your-socks-off handsome. That wasn't why I loved him, though. His looks were just frosting on the cake.

"We need to talk." I walked inside his well-appointed

domain. I'd never been inside his place before. Since the divorce, I'd done my best to avoid him and he'd cooperated by staying away from me and the places I frequented.

His place was stunning, all done up in beige and brown with touches of black. Lots of glass, no knick-knacks. A man's home.

I would bet dollars to donuts he'd hired a decorator. "Come sit down." He indicated the saddle-tan leather sofa, then the wood-and-glass coffee table fronting it. "Sorry about the mess."

I studied the boxy-looking device he indicated on the table. It had a small screen on one side and two slots on the other. In front of it, connected by a spiral cord, was a keyboard. To one side sat some kind of printer.

"What is that?"

"It's a portable computer," he said with satisfaction. "I brought it home to learn how to use it."

"It doesn't look all that portable to me."

"Only eighteen pounds," he said proudly. "The first computers filled a big room. They've come a long way since then."

"What does it do?"

"It processes words that can be edited and printed out." He indicated the printer. "I write on it with the keyboard. But you didn't come here to talk about computers. Since you've never been here before, my guess is that something has happened."

"Yes." I would have loved to avoid this conversation longer, but knew I'd have to tell him sooner or later.

"Sounds serious."

"It is. Could I have a glass of water?" I needed to ease my dry throat so I could say things I didn't want to say.

"Coming right up."

Water in hand, I tried to remember my plan of revelation. Not too abrupt, lead up to it—

"Johnny, Laura is pregnant."

He recoiled against the couch, his mouth opening in protest, his expression disbelieving. "She's just a baby. Are you sure?"

"She was born in 1967, which makes her sixteen."

"Sixteen!" He didn't seem able to take it in and rose to his feet, then sat down again. "Laurie's my little girl. She'd never—I mean, she'd never let a boy—"

"Like her mother wouldn't," I interrupted. I wanted to shout *We made a baby, too!* I'd kept those words locked away too long and they never came out.

His face twisted into ugly lines I didn't recognize. "I swear to God, I'll kill the kid who did this to her."

"No, you won't. He's a stupid boy who made a mistake, just as Laura is a nice girl who messed up. Just as her parents messed up."

He groaned. "We're lucky we didn't get caught in that trap. I tried to be careful."

Careful? Not careful enough, unfortunately. If Johnny, who'd longed for a son like nearly every other man on the planet, knew I'd given away our baby boy, it would kill him. It had almost killed me.

For a few tense moments, our gazes locked. It took effort to shake off the power of his stare. "We have to think what to do," I said.

"Yeah, I guess. Why isn't she here with you?"

"She's ashamed to face you. She didn't like me finding out, either. She was crying this morning and eventually told me." *Tell him! Tell him now what I did all those years ago.*

He didn't wait for me to continue. "I'm her father!" He shouted the words. "Doesn't she trust me to—" His voice cracked. "I should have been there, Frankie. This is my fault."

"No, it's not. You've spent lots of time with the girls."

"But I wasn't *there,* in the house, checking out the teenage scumbags hanging around."

'She didn't hang out with scumbags. If anyone's to blame, it's me. I obviously wasn't paying as much attention as I should."

He caught my hands in his. "Frankie, you've raised those girls mostly alone. Yeah, I know it was your choice, but I should have picked you up and carried you off to a cave somewhere and kept you there until you came to your senses."

I managed a shaky laugh. "I don't think that would have worked."

"Why? Because you stopped loving me?"

In the stillness of the room, I could hear his breathing, feel my own deepen. "Johnny," I said at last, "I never stopped loving you."

"And I never stopped loving you and our kids, the life we had together until you…did what you did."

My hands stiffened in his. "Until what *I* did?" Did he know? He *couldn't* know that I'd given up our first child for adoption.

"Don't look like you're about to go into shock," he said. "What you did was make up your mind about me on circumstantial evidence. Do you remember I told you I'd never cheat on you again? I kept that promise, no matter how it might have looked."

I jerked away and stood up. "Why are we talking about the past? We need to talk about Laura, not us."

"We are. Laura needs two parents and so does Katy, and by God, they're going to *have* two parents."

"That's not something you can decide alone."

"I'll talk you into it." He grabbed me by the hips and pulled me down onto his lap. "When were you happiest, Frankie, with me or on your own? When were the girls happiest?"

"You know the answer to that." I felt paralyzed, unable even to struggle.

"Then why are we torturing each other?"

"I...I don't know." The scene in San Diego seemed so long ago and far away. I hadn't taken time to think back then, and I'd avoided thinking about it since.

To my astonishment, he lifted me off his lap and plunked me down on the couch. He looked directly into my eyes. "Okay, then, here's what we'll do for Laura. We'll get married, go home and handle this together— handle *everything* together, now and in the future."

I stopped breathing. "We can't do that."

"Why not? You said you love me."

"Yes, but—"

"And I love you."

"That's what you said, but—"

"And you know now, in your heart, that you screwed up last time, just as I screwed up the first time."

"Yes, I know all that, but—" I was astonished by the admission and stopped short.

"So what's your problem?"

I opened my mouth to protest and instead said what I really thought. "We should never have divorced in the first place. Make that the second place."

"I'm astonished you'd admit it."

"I admit it, all right? This thing is...how will we

ever explain getting married for the third time? We'll be the joke of Newton County."

He exploded with laughter. "That is so like you, Frankie. What the hell do we have to explain? Who the hell do we have to explain it to? Grow up, girl! You'll never be happy without me." His eyes narrowed and his smile widened. "Didn't you realize that when you went out with old Harold?"

"How did you know about Harold?"

"I have my ways. I heard he made you cry."

I stared at him, openmouthed. If everybody doesn't know your business, Mother used to say, you're not living in a small town.

He kept pushing. "Is Harold your ideal man?"

"Are you kidding?"

"Have you met any guys you like more than me?"

"Such guys don't exist." I felt myself falling into the hole he was digging at my feet.

"I love you," he said. "Please notice what I said first— I love you, even though you can really make me see red at times. Now I'm asking you a question. Will you marry me, Frankie? Immediately, before you change your mind and I have to convince you all over again?"

I felt weak as a wet washrag, as limp as a deflated balloon. How could I possibly say yes to him again? I couldn't do that.

"Yes " I shouted it at him. "I'll marry you, Johnny Davis!" I tried to throw myself into his arms but he held me back.

"There's a second question involved here."

"Ask it!"

"Will you promise to trust me from this day forward? No matter what happens, will you promise?"

I made the promise so easily that later, I wondered what he'd put in my water.

JOHNNY CANCELED my return flight to Kansas City, then called the Cook County clerk's office to find out about a marriage license. We'd have to go to the vital records division of a county building to get one; unfortunately, we'd have to wait until the next day to marry.

"No problem," Johnny assured me. "I know a judge who'll do the honors. Now I'm going to have to make a lot of telephone calls, set everything up for me to leave the business in good hands. Do you mind the delay?"

I shook my head, realizing I was in a state of shock with little rational thought left. I hadn't come here to marry the man, for heaven's sake. I hadn't dared imagine such a thing could ever happen again.

"Then let's take off." He grabbed my hand and led me toward the door. "We'll go to the county building on Clark Street and do what has to be done."

He stopped short and my momentum carried me into his arms.

"I love you, Frankie."

"I love—"

His kiss interrupted my words, his lips strong and masterful against mine. One of us knew what we were doing, obviously. I clung to him and kissed him back, just as I always had.

I'd put my life in his hands again and I felt more secure than I could remember being for a very long time.

FOR THE THIRD go-round, we married with the wedding rings he'd bought in Las Vegas so long ago. Would the third time be a charm?

I surprised him by presenting the Vegas silver dollar that I'd been carrying around in my wallet for years.

"This really is like starting over from the beginning," he said, grinning at the coin. "I don't know about you, but I feel like a newlywed."

"So do I, Johnny."

"Let's go home and celebrate," he said, adding quickly, "I mean my place, not Missouri."

"Thank heaven!" I teased him. "I was wondering about your patience."

"I don't have any," he said. "Let's get out of here and do our thing!"

And that's what we did. We spent the rest of the day and all night in bed, discovering each other all over again. Life was good once more.

WHEN WE DROVE UP to the house the day following the ceremony, Katy came running, her ponytail bouncing.

"Daddy!" She flung her eleven-year-old self into his arms. "I love you, Daddy!"

"I love you, too." He lifted her off her feet and swung her around, her feet flying through the air along with her giggles.

Glancing up, I saw Laura standing behind the screen door. She made no effort to join us.

Johnny set Katy back on her feet and she held his hand. Glancing at me, she said, "You, too, Mom. I love you!"

"Ditto."

I blew her a kiss and started for the house. Behind me, I heard her say, "Are you gonna stay, Daddy? I want you to stay for a loooong time. Will you?"

Laura opened the screen door and walked out onto

the porch. She wore a pink T-shirt and shorts that revealed her long, tan legs. Overall, she looked tired and miserable.

"Don't be a dweeb," she said to her sister in cutting tones. "He never stays very long."

"And hello to you, too, Laura," Johnny said in a teasing tone. "You gonna come hug your old dad?"

Laura did not move and I recognized her expression. She was revved up for a fight.

Unknowing, Katy frowned and hung on to his shirt-tail. "You're mean!" she accused her sister. "Daddy, *will* you stay a long time?"

Johnny patted her head, but he was looking at Laura. "I'll stay forever," he said. He held up his left hand, the golden band catching the light. "Your mother and I got married. What do you think of that?"

Katy let out a hysterical shriek and began jumping up and down with delight. Laura's jaw dropped and she stared for a moment, then took a step forward.

"Is it true?" She looked from him to me and back again. Tears slid down her cheeks. "I've dreamed this so many times but I never thought—"

Johnny disentangled himself from Katy and walked to the bottom of the steps. Looking up at Laura, he said, "I'm sorry I ever left, honey. I won't make that mistake again."

For a moment, the girl hesitated and then she hurtled down the steps and into his open arms.

I turned away, my eyes blurred with tears. This was my fault because I'd kept them apart. Seeing them together did more to heal my spirit than anything else ever could.

CHAPTER SIXTEEN

LAURA LOST her baby ten days after our return. She lay in my arms weeping, a very young girl who'd suffered a difficult solution to an age-old problem. So much for the conversations about "what's best for Laura." So much for Johnny's determination to get her to reveal the name of the father.

"It will be all right," I said, trying to soothe her. "The doctor says this was a very clean miscarriage." Actually, he'd said it was a clean spontaneous abortion but I knew that the word *abortion* would upset Laura even more.

I rubbed her shoulders. "You're young and healthy and you'll have other babies."

"No, I won't! I'll never let another boy get near me as long as I live," she sobbed. "He doesn't even care!"

"He doesn't know you lost the baby, honey." I stroked her shoulders, smoothed back her hair. "Did you tell him you were even pregnant?"

"N-no, but he should have known. He just said I was acting like a doofus and never even tried to find out why."

"Did you want him to know?"

"No!"

"You just wanted him to care."

"Yes."

"Baby, I know it hurts and this is hard, but it's better this way. Nobody knows except you, me, Dad and the doctor. I realize how scary and difficult this is for you, but you'll be your old self very soon. According to the doctor—"

"What does the doctor know? I never want to go through this again. No kids for me, ever."

"Now you don't mean that. This is an incredibly traumatic experience. You'll change your mind, in time."

"I won't." She sat up, her lower lip thrust out stubbornly. Long, tangled blond hair spilled over her shoulders. "He told me he wouldn't get me pregnant. He *promised*."

"Laura, baby, nobody can look out for you except you. You know about birth control—we've talked about it. Part of the responsibility is yours."

Her head dropped. "I trusted him," she whispered.

"I know. But you won't make that mistake again."

She raised her gaze and her lips curled scornfully. "I've learned my lesson. I'm through with boys forever. The thing is, I went through all this hell and it wasn't even that much fun to begin with."

I wanted to laugh with relief but controlled myself. "When everything's right, it *will* be fun. Trust me on that. But you must grow up and wait for a man you love, not some sex-crazed teenager who sells you a line."

"I'll wait forever." She gave a prodigious yawn. "What did Doc give me in that pill?"

"Just something to help you rest. Lie back and let it work."

She rubbed her beautiful blue eyes. "Okay. Tell Daddy...tell Daddy that..."

I knew what to tell Daddy, who was waiting in the living room to make sure his child was on the mend. I found him staring out the window, his brow wrinkled.

"She's fine," I said. "This is all but over. Doc says there'll be no physical aftermath. Mentally, she hates men, but that will pass, too."

"Will it?" He turned to face me. "I don't think it ever passed for you."

Astonished, I stared at him. "What in the world are you talking about?"

"You. *Hate* may be too strong a word, but you sure don't trust them...us...whoever."

"I'm a very trustful person." Hurt, I frowned at him. Even so, I had to wonder deep in my heart, was he right? Was I suspicious and doubtful or, as my father always said, did I holler before I was hurt?

"That was before," I said at last. "I told you I've changed."

"I'm counting on that because I love you more than anyone in the world loves you, or ever will." He stepped closer and put his arms around me. "If you can't trust me now, everything we have, everything we had, is over and done with. We don't want Laura to pick up on that particular hang-up, Frankie. We've got to help her get past all this."

"Yes, Johnny." I said it meekly, trying to process what he had said. Was I really suspicious and doubtful? I would prove him wrong this time.

"YOU TWO DONE it again?"

I heard that question so often that I finally put up a

sign in Reva's: *Yes, we done it again.* Johnny laughed at me, but concurred it was a good idea.

We settled back into family life as if it had never been disrupted. Johnny's influence on the girls was incredible. Everyone, including me, brightened up. Soon they were going to him with their questions and problems and I welcomed the reprieve.

Johnny and Laura came to me the spring of her senior year with such serious faces that I knew I should have been paying more attention. "Should I sit down?" I asked.

Johnny said, "Good idea."

We sat around the kitchen table and I looked from one to the other with rising dread. "Somebody say something," I urged.

Johnny leaned back in his chair. "Laura, this is your show. Start talking."

Laura sucked in a deep breath, her face the picture of determination. "Mom, I'm not going to college in the fall."

"What!" I straightened. "Of course you are. We've done all the paperwork and made all the plans—"

"I know. I would have told you earlier, but it took me a while to make up my mind. The thing is, I've been talking to Dad and thinking about this and—"

"What!" I sounded like a broken record and gave Johnny a shocked glance.

"Take it easy," he urged. "There was no need to say anything to you until she was sure about what she wanted to do. Why get you upset before we had to?"

"I had no idea… What brought this on, Laura?"

She looked down at her fingers spread wide on the tabletop. "I just need some time," she said. "I'll take one year off and then go to college the next year. I promise."

"No, you won't. You take one year off and it'll be twice as hard to go back to school. Don't you know how important education is to your future?"

"You didn't go to college."

"Because I already had my future planned out. You don't."

"That's why I need some time. If I went to college right after high school, I'd be fumbling around and trying to figure out why I was there. I can do that on my own time, for free."

I pursed my lips. "If you think you can take a year to sit around and meditate—"

She laughed, almost as if relieved. "I've already got a job. It's with a women's crisis center in Tulsa. Aunt Eileen fixed it up for me. She says I can stay with her. This will give me a chance to find out if I really want to become a social worker, which is what I'm leaning toward."

"Oh, my God." Helplessly I looked at her sitting there so confident in her choice, apparently waiting for me to lose my temper. "I thought you wanted to major in education," I said at last.

"There are other ways to help children than as a teacher," she said, her voice soft.

In a flash, I understood—the pregnancy. It had changed her life completely, forced her to grow up faster than she would have otherwise. She saw a mission in her life now, a mission to help others. "Oh, honey—"

"It'll be okay. You spent some time with Aunt Eileen when you were about my age, didn't you?"

That jolted me and I nodded. I didn't like being pulled back to that time.

"See?" She spoke triumphantly. "You didn't go to college. You came back home and worked at Grandma's and married Daddy."

It sure sounded simple the way she told it.

"Did Grandma object?"

"No, but—"

"But nothing, Mom." Laura leaned forward on her elbows. "I know what I'm doing. I swear I'm not planning to waste a year. This is very important to me."

I turned toward Johnny. "And you?"

He shrugged. "Honey, she's an adult. She can vote, according to the twenty-sixth amendment of the constitution. She can join the army. She's a sensible girl who has given this long, hard thought."

He reached across and cupped my hand with his. "It's her decision, not ours. We can support her and guide her but in the end—"

"Okay, I get it." I looked down at his strong tanned hand covering mine. "I still wish I'd heard about this before everything was decided."

Laura nodded. "I know, and I'm sorry, but I just wasn't up to fighting it out with you. I knew Daddy would be calm." She rose. "Thank you both for being so understanding."

I gave her a wry smile. "I'm trying."

IN BED THAT NIGHT, Johnny took me in his arms and kissed my temple. "You mad at me?" he asked. "About Laura, I mean."

I sighed. "No. I guess not. It was a surprise, though."

"She doesn't plan to marry some idiot kid and become a hippie."

That made me laugh. "There are still a few weirdos

out there, but the flower children have drifted away along with pet rocks and mood rings."

"Sad but true. Or maybe not so sad at all. They never quite managed to change the world, just scare it to death."

The silence stretched out and finally I said into the darkness, "Okay, Johnny, what is it you're not telling me?"

"Welll…I've got this idea."

I braced myself. "Lay it on me."

"I'm thinking that I may offer Jeff a job. Or maybe I should call it a career."

"My brother Jeff?"

"What other Jeff would I be talking about?"

"Good point. Why?"

"Because he's grown into a pretty smart guy."

"Really?" To me he was just my middle sibling. "Has he given up that rock band dream?"

"Yeah. What I was thinking…" He abruptly changed directions. "You know how much time I spend running back and forth to Chicago."

"I know it all too well."

"I'm thinking if I brought in someone I could trust to back me up in Chicago, maybe I could cut back on those trips. I could train him to move up in the organization."

"Do you mean it?" I rolled over on top of him. "That would be great!"

"I think so, too." He slid a hand to the small of my back and pressed down gently. "Jeff's been all over the country playing music. In between gigs, he's worked all kinds of jobs—sales, manual labor, you name it."

"And these are qualifications for running car dealerships?"

"Why not? I could start him in sales and let him work his way up until he's my assistant."

"I don't know. He's always been so fancy-free. What makes you think he'd want to stay in Chicago?"

"The fact that it's his wife's hometown."

"His wife!" I beat his chest with my fists. "What else are you not telling me?"

"Have mercy!" Laughing, he caught my fists in his big hands. "He called about an hour ago, while you were in the bathtub. Once he gave me the news, I started thinking." He pulled my hands to his mouth and kissed both of them. "This is the first chance we've had to talk."

"Okay," I grumbled. "I forgive you."

"He's already in Chicago so he won't even have to move. What do you think?"

"I think you're the greatest guy in the world and Jeff's wife will probably like you even more than I do."

"Like?" He grabbed my shoulders and pulled me down onto his chest.

"Love," I amended. "Love you. So show me some action, buster!"

He did, with enthusiasm.

JEFF JUMPED at the chance to join the Davis automobile family. His wife, Kayla, liked the offer even more than he did.

"It was so wonderful of Johnny to think of him," she enthused while basting the turkey that Thanksgiving. "He is absolutely the nicest man."

"He ain't bad," I said with a smile.

Kayla nodded, her curly dark hair bobbing. "You're wonderful, too. Thanks for inviting us for Thanksgiving."

"I'm giving thanks that my brother found you," I

said in all honesty. "And I'm thankful he's willing to settle down to a regular steady job."

"Me, too." Kayla's cheeks, reddened by the warmth from that twenty-five-pound turkey, reddened even more. "He has to settle down, whether he wants to or not," she said, "because we're going to have a baby in six months or so."

"Congratulations!" I gave her a big hug. "You must both be so thrilled."

"We are. When I see your daughter I get even more excited. Katy's a great kid. How old is she?"

"She's thirteen. I'm sorry Laura couldn't be here, but she's volunteering at a soup kitchen."

Johnny popped his head through the door, sniffing appreciatively at the aroma of turkey and pumpkin pie. "We're starving out here," he complained. "Any snacks hanging around?"

"Veggies and dip in the fridge," I told him. "Dinner will be on the table in an hour or so."

"I'm giving thanks for that." He dug out the tray and carried it back into the family room where everyone waited. There was Johnny, Jeff, Katy, her friend Kevin, Johnny's mother, Dorothy, her reasonably new husband Leif, Joanie and even Carrie the big newspaper columnist.

And for all of this, I gave thanks, too.

AFTER OUR EARLY holiday dinner, the women and I took off for Reva's and the community-wide Thanksgiving banquet for those without other plans, or who were less fortunate. We'd done this for years, way back when Mother was in charge, but there was always a modest stipend to cover costs for those who could pay.

This year, however, Johnny footed the bill. Back at the house parked in front of television football games with the rest of the men, he'd promised they'd come down later and help out.

My sister-in-law, Mindy, had come in early to get the turkeys into the oven. Most of the other fixings we'd prepared ahead. Now, with all our new recruits, we pitched in and opened the doors at three.

Carrie paused beside me, her face damp with perspiration and her eyes glowing. She was following in the footsteps of Lois Lane and loving it.

She slipped an arm around my waist. "This is fabulous," she said, looking around at the overflowing tables and chairs. "Johnny's great to do this."

"Johnny's great? Where is he?" I looked about with exaggerated interest. "I don't see him anywhere around mopping up tables or carrying trays."

She laughed. "Okay, I should also add that we women aren't doing too shabby a job, either. Especially Jeff's wife. She's working like a dog."

"And loving every minute of it," I added, watching Kayla serve plates to a table of old-timers. "Jeff got lucky when he found her."

"I think you got lucky when you found Johnny."

I let out an exasperated sigh. "Why doesn't anyone tell him how lucky he was to find *me*."

Hands settled on my shoulders, making me jump. Johnny said, "Nobody has to tell me I'm lucky because I know."

Laughing, I leaned back against him. "Don't sneak up on me that way! You may hear something you'd rather avoid."

"I'll take my chances." He kissed my ear. "Hey, I ran into old Mrs. Kelly on my way in."

I nodded. "She just finished eating."

"Seems she's got some trouble with a leaky pipe. I told her I'd go take a look at it. Should be a piece of cake."

I turned around so I could give him a hug. "That's really nice of you, honey."

He shrugged. "It's no big deal. I'll be back later for another piece of pumpkin pie."

"You got it." I watched him walk to the door, his tall, broad-shouldered body weaving between the tables.

Carrie was right. I *was* lucky.

JOHNNY'S GOOD DEED for Mrs. Kelly soon blossomed into a part-time volunteer job. I began to think that every little old lady in the county knew he was a soft touch. He didn't mind, and with Jeff in Chicago, Johnny had more time of his own now.

Christmas came and went. When I was a kid, it always felt as if around the holidays time stood still. Christmas seemed to come only once every five years, and the same with my birthday. Now time passed in a flash with special milestones speeding by along the way.

Laura didn't come home from Tulsa as often as I'd have liked. When she did, though, she looked and sounded like a different person—a different woman. After the hugs and the kisses, we sat together and she told us about her time away from home.

"I can't stress enough how much this has affected me," she said. "I know now, for sure, that I want to be a licensed social worker, and perhaps even a therapist. There are so many women out there who need assistance. My biggest frustration was being more or less a gofer, when I wanted to dig in and do some real good."

Johnny patted her hand. "Your time will come, baby. I take it you're going back to school in the fall?"

She nodded. "I'm going to stay year-round so I can finish, then get my master's as quickly as possible." She looked at me and suddenly smiled. "Are you surprised, Mom?"

"Not at all. I'm proud."

Even Katy was proud. She told me later that she was quite impressed with her sister's dedication.

"I thought she'd be, like, a lawyer or something big like that," she said.

"How about you? What do you want to be when you grow up?"

She made a face at me and laughed. Shorter than Laura and not as blond, Katy was a real fireball with blue eyes like her father's and thick, shiny brown hair.

"Maybe I'll be a gym teacher," she mused. "Or maybe I'll go to the Olympics. Or—"

"What in the world would you go to the Olympics for?" I teased her. "Is talking on the phone an event?"

She shrugged. "Not that I know of. Maybe I'll try...fencing."

"With swords? I don't think so."

"Good point. Okay, I know how to swim. I could do that."

"Sure, if you practice eight hours a day for five or six years. Do you remember your brush with the swim team? Once you found out they met at the pool at 5:00 a.m. to swim laps, you bailed."

"Yeah, I guess I have to think about that." She jumped up, gave me a quick kiss and took off for parts unknown. God, life was good when we were all together.

CHAPTER SEVENTEEN

KATY AND LAURA graduated in 1990, one from high school and the other from college. Johnny and I ran from one ceremony to the other, incredibly proud of our girls.

Laura never missed a step. She started a new job with the social services department of San Antonio almost immediately.

"Don't you want at least a little vacation?" I asked. "We've missed you, Laura."

"I don't have time. Lots to do, Mom."

She intended to change the world. I hoped she could, but if not, I hoped it didn't break her heart. I'd known others with the same "change the world" plan and I'd seen how that went.

Katy was already enrolled at the University of Missouri for the fall term. "I've got to have some fun this summer," she told me, sounding restless. "Be prepared. Daddy gave me that new convertible for graduation and I intend to put many miles on it."

Johnny shook his head. "Katy, your *parents* gave you that car."

"Wherever it came from, I love it." She blew kisses and skipped out of the room.

Johnny and I looked at each other and burst out laughing. Our girls were moving on, but we still had each other.

KATY SPENT TWO YEARS in college and then informed us she was not going back; she was getting married.

"You're too young," I wailed, realizing immediately that I sounded just like my mother.

"I'm older than you were when you first got married," she reminded me smugly.

"Times were different then. You're also too educated."

"How many years did you spend in college, Mother?" Her tone was far too sweet.

"Like I said, it was different back then. Besides, I knew what my life would be like and I'd already been trained for it by my mother. I wanted to marry your father and stay here to take over Reva's when the time came."

"How about you, Dad?"

"I dropped out and joined the marine corps."

I gave him an approving glance. Hippie adventures and drug dalliances were not something you wanted to share with your kid.

Johnny looked at her sternly. "When are we going to meet this guy you're planning to get hitched with?"

"Tomorrow. He's driving up from Little Rock."

I rolled my eyes. "What on earth is he doing in Little Rock?"

"Working for his father, who owns a computer business. They make…" She frowned. "Sooner or later, I've got to put some effort into learning about computer stuff. I think it's called…peripherals?"

"Girl, you wouldn't know a peripheral if it spit in your eye," I announced. "But then, neither would I."

Her grin sparkled. "That's okay. He doesn't love me for my brain."

Turned out, Doug Tripp thought Katy walked on

water. When he looked at her, he practically melted. A tall, handsome young man, he shook hands with her father and declared his love. "I've never known anyone like her," he concluded.

Johnny raised his eyebrows. "I don't doubt that for a minute."

I could barely keep from laughing. After Doug left, Katy ambushed us. "Well? What do you think? Isn't he great? Isn't he cute?"

"Yes," I said, "he's great and he's cute and he has good manners."

"You judged him on manners?" She looked appalled. "Daddy? What did you think?"

"I think if he ever finds out you don't really own a halo he'll die of shock. Katy, that guy thinks you're made of sugar and spice—and so do I."

"That's what Mom's made of," she said stubbornly, "and I'm just like her."

"God forbid," Johnny and I said in unison, then started laughing. I added, "I hope you don't plan to get married anytime soon."

"Heavens, no. We're thinking around Labor Day."

"Of which year?"

"This one."

"What? We couldn't even plan a decent elopement in that amount of time. It's just a few months away!"

"We can do it," she said with utter confidence. "And I want it to be big. I mean *big*. I want you to make my dress—"

"How can I do that and still plan this wedding?"

"I'll plan the wedding," Johnny offered. "We'll invite everyone in town, hold it at the bandstand and serve southern fried chicken and beer."

"Daddy!" She gave him a light tap on the chest. "We've got to do better than that. I know *exactly* what I want and it's all got to be *perfect*."

Johnny and I looked at each other with dread.

"Look at the bright side," he said. "She'll get married and move to Arkansas and we'll be finished with our parental duties. It'll just be you and me, babe. Just you and me."

EVERYTHING WENT WRONG at Katy's wedding and the "it must be perfect" girl could not have cared less. The flowers were late, the dress was creased from hanging in the closet, some kid took a swath of frosting off the wedding cake but still her smile never wavered.

Before the happy couple departed for their honeymoon, Katy gave me an enormous hug and whispered in my ear, "Thank you, Mom. You and Dad are the best parents in the world." She kissed my cheek. "I hope you two will try to make it last this time."

Openmouthed, I watched her scurry away to tell her father goodbye.

EVERYONE CAME for Christmas that year and for many after that. Johnny and I couldn't have been happier with our loved ones around us. Laura, alone but beautiful and happy with her job. Katy and her husband, Doug, and after their first three years of marriage, their twin babies.

That particular Christmas was a special thrill. Katy cooked the holiday dinner, improving on the recipes I'd taught her in childhood.

"You just sit and relax, Mom," she informed me. "You

do enough cooking as it is." She smiled happily. "Besides, I enjoy it." She winked. "And I want to impress Doug."

Laura chimed in. "I'll help her—with dinner, not with Doug. I'm not that much of a cook, compared to you two, but I can assist. Tell me what to do and I take orders quite well."

I was glad to fall in with their plans. My girls delighted me, and never more than during holidays. Carrying my glass of wine, I joined the men and the babies in the family room.

I sat there silently, enjoying the voices, the giggles of the kids. After a while, Johnny said to me, "What are you doing, honey?"

"Being happy," I said, my heart bursting with joy. "Merry Christmas, everyone! I love you all."

They looked at me as if I were crazy, all except Johnny, who smiled and mouthed the words, *I love you, too.*

"You really don't need to worry about all these computer updates they're talking about, John," Doug said. "And this new software won't crash and the world won't stop turning. Just unplug everything and go to bed when the time comes and—"

"—this, too, shall pass," I inserted. Everything would pass, the good and the bad. We could only hope the good would pass more slowly. "Besides, it's not coming up for a while."

Later, when all the kids were gone and Johnny and I were alone before a roaring fire, he put his arm around me and kissed the top of my head. "Happy, sweetheart?"

I sighed with contentment. "You know I am. You?"

"Yes. Me, too. Did Laura get a chance to tell you her news?"

"What news?"

"She's found a man who may measure up to her impossible standards. He's one of her supervisors at work so they share the same passion."

"Oh, Johnny, that's wonderful. I knew some day she'd get over…what happened."

"I think that time has finally come."

"Hallelujah." I wasn't even surprised she'd told him instead of me. Laura didn't like being in the spotlight.

I gave Johnny a coquettish smile and added, "I like my new robe." I smoothed my hand down the red velvet he'd given me for Christmas.

"You always like your robe. I get you one every year. They used to be sheer and sexy. Now…" He laughed. "Now I don't need the fancy wrappings, I just need to keep my woman warm."

"Just like every year I get you silk pajamas, which you wear right up to bedtime," I teased, snuggling closer. "I love you, Johnny."

"I love you, Frankie." He tightened his grip. "Next year will be the best ever for us."

I wanted desperately for it to be this way forever. I didn't even mind when a write-in campaign elected him mayor of our little town. No one deserved that recognition more than he.

In fact, I'd rather have him presiding over meetings than running around making repairs for little old ladies, and even ladies not so old.

THE RETURN OF Millicent Robberson set me back on my heels. She'd moved away after Daddy's death, but now she was back in Fairweather with her daughter, Kathy, and teenaged grandson, Max. Millie's health was bad, I heard through the grapevine. Kathy had come along to take care of her, or so it was said.

Max joined them because he had no choice in the matter. A tall, strong boy of fourteen, he immediately set about antagonizing every kid in town and succeeded to an amazing degree.

I hadn't seen the two women since they got back into town, but Max came into Reva's after a couple of weeks and plunked himself down on a stool. He didn't look too appealing, what with the ragged jeans and do-rag on his head. As a matter of fact, I nearly laughed at the sight.

The kid could pass as a hippie without a great deal of trouble.

"Gimme a cheeseburger with everything," he ordered, his chin lifting to an arrogant angle. "And a root beer. Make it snappy because I'm in a hurry."

Lynda took immediate offense and so did I, watching him through the pass-through window over the grill.

Lynda pursed her lips. "When kids talk to me like I'm their servant, I seem to get slower and slower. I don't hear too well, either. Give me your order again and do it nice."

He glared at her. "Just get my food, lady. I'm not here to make friends."

"Good thing, because if you are, it isn't working."

Each held their position and glared at the other. Finally the kid said, "Do I get my food or not?"

"Sure, if you give me the order again and say please."

I came through the kitchen door, all prepared to

play peacemaker. "Now wait a minute, you two. Let's all be friends here."

"I don't want friends, I want food!" The boy looked ready to explode.

At that precise moment, Johnny walked through the front door and stopped short. "What's going on here?" he inquired.

Lynda didn't even look at him, still too busy trying to stare down the kid. "We got us an uncooperative customer here." She pointed to a sign near the cash register. "See that sign, boy? It says we can refuse service to anybody we don't like, and I don't like you."

"Lady, you can go—"

He never finished the sentence because Johnny grabbed him by the neck of his T-shirt and hauled him off the stool. "You and me," he said. "We need to have a little talk."

"Who the hell are you?" the boy blustered. "You've got no right to—"

"I'm the mayor of this town and I can throw your butt into jail in a New York minute." The jail part wasn't true, but the kid didn't know that. "Now calm down and follow me outside."

They marched through the door, the man in charge. Lynda turned to me. "Now why is Johnny doing that? He won't get anywhere with that hoodlum."

I shrugged and went back to the kitchen. I couldn't agree with Lynda less. Knowing Johnny, the kid had just met more than his match.

I PUT THE INCIDENT with Max out of my mind until the rumors started. Johnny had not only tamed the boy, but he'd also come to the aid of Max's mother and grandmother. Millie's house had sat empty for a number of years and now it needed all kinds of work, which the women prevailed upon Johnny to perform.

What he couldn't do himself, he hired others to do.

"Why are you getting all mixed up with that family?" I complained. "I'm not too crazy about this."

"They need all the help they can get, Frankie." He spoke seriously, stirring sugar into his coffee across the counter at Reva's. "They've got no money to speak of, and Millie's sick. I don't know quite what the problem is, but she looks like hell. Kathy's running herself ragged trying to take care of the other two."

"Somebody *ought* to take care of that boy," I muttered. "He's running all over town pissing people off."

"I know, and I'm working on it. He's not a bad kid, but he's never had his father around to set him straight. He just needs a strong hand."

"Which you're providing." I grimaced. "Johnny, you can't take on all the troubles of the world."

"That's not what I'm doing, honey." He tilted his head and frowned. "Is there something more to this that I don't know?"

I heaved a sigh. *I might as well level with him.* "Millie is the woman my dad was playing around with," I said tightly. "I don't think she deserves help from my family."

"I see." He drained his mug and put it down. "I understand how you feel, but I'm going to do what I think is right. I've made mistakes, too, as you well know. I hope I've got past the point where it's thrown in my face again."

He slid off the stool. "You're the only person I know who's without a past blemish," he said with a sarcastic edge I'd never heard before. "Sorry, babe, but I've got to satisfy my own conscience."

He flipped a salute and ambled out. I stood there, feeling uneasy for many different reasons.

JOHNNY WENT ON his way, and apparently he actually *was* doing a lot of good. Soon it got to the point where Max followed him like a shadow, but Johnny didn't tell me that, gossip did. All I knew firsthand was that when he came to Reva's, Max was a new kid. He spoke politely and cast Johnny quick glances seeking approval.

Everyone commented on the change in the boy. Me? I stayed out of it. I couldn't warm to that family, but I could still be polite.

Johnny never spoke of them to me, but then, he never spoke of the others he assisted, either. He might say, "I put an old fence back up today," but he'd never say for whom he did it. And I didn't ask.

He did mention when graffiti turned up on the front of city hall.

"The police department assumes it's kids," he said, stirring his coffee.

"Seems logical." An obvious thought struck me. "You don't suppose it's—"

"Don't even say it!" He leaned forward, his expression full of warning. "That kid gets blamed for everything that goes wrong in this town and I'm sick of it."

"Don't get on your high horse," I advised. "It was just a passing thought." And although I didn't say it, I'd heard suspicions about the boy before from others.

"Yeah, right." He threw down his napkin. "Frankie, you're getting just like the rest of the people in this town."

"Meaning what?" Offended, I stared at him.

"Meaning you listen to gossip and, even worse, you believe it."

"Why are you in such an uproar? I just suggested the obvious. If you say Max is innocent, I believe you."

"Then that's what I say!" Shoving back his chair, he stomped out of the house.

What in the world was going on with him? I'd never known him to get so bent out of shape about other people's business. Maybe I'd better start paying a little bit more attention to the time he spent with Max.

A sudden thought struck me. A boy. As the father of two girls, he'd never had a chance to guide a boy. Was that the appeal here?

I chewed on my lip, feeling guilty all over again. He had a son, of course, but he didn't know it. I had prayed that my guilt for keeping that son from him would lessen over the years.

I'd been so very wrong.

VOWING NEVER TO mention Max to Johnny again, still, I couldn't help being curious about the vandalism that continued throughout the town. This was unusual for Fairweather, but then, everything seemed to be changing. Snug little hamlets such as this one could no longer hide from the great big world out there. And it showed. Old customs such as civility seemed to be sliding into history. New customs such as insolence and bad language crashed right in to fill the void.

"Somebody smashed into the grocery store last night," Lynda reported one morning. "I heard it from my cousin, Dennis. You remember him—he's on the force."

I nodded. "How much damage was done?"

"Just that big front window, but a lot of stuff was taken—beer mostly, and snacks."

"Does he think it's the same person or persons who's been doing all the other vandalism around town?"

Lynda shrugged. "Dennis didn't say. I'll bet it is, though. And if it's not that Robberson kid, I'll pay for lying."

"Now, Lynda, you don't know that. You just don't like him."

"You got that right." She gathered empty glasses off the counter. "But you mark my words, sooner or later that kid will be in jail where he belongs."

Johnny heard that kind of talk, too, and came home that night in a foul mood. "Max can't walk down the street without somebody pointing to him and whispering," he said. "I'm trying to convince him that it's worth his while to become a law-abiding citizen and this isn't helping."

He glared at me. "Don't you have anything to say?"

"Why would I? You'd just get mad, or perhaps I should say madder. I don't want to get involved."

"I thought you were going to be more trusting," he groused. "Isn't that what you said that day you came to Chicago?"

"I said I would trust *you*. I'll try to extend the same courtesy to the rest of the world, but you're my top priority." I kissed his cheek. "I trust you. There. If you say the boy is innocent, I believe you, but I won't talk about it to anybody else. So will you please calm down?"

He did eventually, but the whole situation made me uneasy. He might be sure of Max, but I certainly wasn't, despite what I said. I had no reason to think him guilty of the current crop of misdemeanors…but I had no reason to think him innocent, either.

CHAPTER EIGHTEEN

A FEW WEEKS LATER, a crisis in the Kansas City car dealership sent Johnny on another trip. I kissed him goodbye and wished him well, then took off for the café. We had a busy day until midafternoon when an enormous noise shook the place.

Everyone in Reva's heard it. We all crowded around the front door and windows, trying to figure out what was going on.

A police car wailed past, followed by an ambulance. Most of the men inside the café rushed outside to follow the emergency vehicles. The women were slower to join them.

I placed a hand over my wildly beating heart. "What on earth do you suppose that was?"

"Some kinda bomb." Lynda shrugged. "I'll bet it's that same creepy kid who's been doing all the other stuff."

"Anything's possible." I hesitated, undecided. Glancing around, I realized that the café was empty. "Look, you stay here and hold the fort and I'll go see what's going on. Okay?"

She frowned. "Okay, if you promise to come right back here and tell me everything."

"You got it." I yanked off my apron and took off after everybody else.

The trail ended at the damaged back door of the bank a few blocks away. Police kept gawkers back and away from the building's crumbled back wall and the cloud of dust and gravel that spun through the air.

I found myself standing next to my old friend Ron Baker. "What's going on?" I gasped, still out of breath from the trot over here.

"Not sure." He peered at the officers on the scene. "Hey, Dennis! Come over here a minute."

Dennis, Lynda's cousin, waved his acknowledgment and in a few minutes joined us.

"Catch the guy who did this?" Ron asked.

"Naw, not yet." Dennis glanced around, then added, "We got a lead, though."

"Somebody saw something?" Not Max, I prayed. With Johnny out of town, the kid wouldn't have any support.

Dennis pointed. "That kid over there on the bicycle says he saw the whole thing."

Ron frowned. "That's Bobby Everett."

Dennis nodded. "We're gonna take him in for questioning."

"What caused the blast?" I asked, watching the firemen at work.

"Homemade bomb is our early guess." Dennis shook his head in disapproval. "Probably a Molotov cocktail," he added officiously. "Anybody can find out how to make one from the library." He turned away. "Gotta get back to work, folks."

Ron and I exchanged knowing glances and he said, "They'll get him this time, sure as shootin'. And if it ain't that Max kid, I'll eat my hat."

"Let's not jump to conclusions," I cautioned, although part of me agreed with him a hundred percent. "Let's wait and see what happens."

WE DIDN'T HAVE long to wait. Within a couple of hours, the word spread all over town: that wild Max kid did it. Bobby had been riding by on his bike and saw him run away. The cops just had to pick Max up and his escalating antics would be over.

My heart sank with the news. This would kill Johnny, who'd placed so much faith in the kid. Should I call him with the bad news?

No, I decided it was better to let him find out in person when he got back.

BY THE TIME Johnny reached home Sunday evening, the police had gone to arrest Max and he hadn't been home. His mother said he was visiting a friend. His grandmother said he was out of town. Someone else said Max had been down by the creek, hiding in the brush.

That was all the town needed to know. People didn't hide unless they were guilty. This time the law would make an example out of him, and most people thought it was high time.

I got so tired of all the phone calls about the incident that I considered not answering anymore, but I couldn't do that. If Max got busted, Johnny should know. What a debacle.

Johnny rolled up to the house at dusk. "Good trip," he said, hauling out his suitcase. "Dad may be getting old but he's still got all his marbles. He has his eye on—"

He stopped short. "What's going on?" he demanded. "You've got that *look* on your face again."

I clutched my hands together. "Johnny, I don't want to be the one to tell you this."

"You're scaring me, Frankie. Let's have it."

"Someone threw a homemade bomb at the back of the bank. The police think it was Max, but so far no one's been able to find him."

He stared at me with his mouth hanging open. "You're saying the cops are after *Max?*"

I nodded. "I'd give anything not to have to tell you all this, but he was seen at the bank by a kid going by on a bicycle right when the bomb went off. Max has been spotted around town since, but the authorities haven't been able to catch him yet."

While I spoke, Johnny's face hardened and an eerie calm settled over him.

"It wasn't Max," he said in a hard, sure voice.

"Oh, Johnny, he was identified. I know this hurts, but your faith in him was misplaced. Surely you see that now?"

He spoke slowly, enunciating every syllable. "It… was…not…Max."

"How can you be so sure when you were out of town?"

"Would you believe me if I swore that I know for a fact that Max didn't do it? Would you trust me that much?"

"I…" Would I? Did I? Johnny's faith in the boy was taking him way out on a limb. "Have you been in touch with him since you got back? Have you seen him since you got back? Did he tell you he was innocent?"

"We're not talking about what anybody told me. We're talking about what *I say.*"

A cold shiver ran through me. I wanted to believe

him, but I just couldn't. I took a deep breath. "If you want me to say yes, I will."

"I want you to say how you really feel."

"Then… Oh, Johnny, ask me again after you get the facts. I was there, at the crime scene, so to speak. I listened to the policemen, I saw the damage to the building."

"You didn't see Max."

"No, I didn't. As far as I know, nobody's seen Max all day. But the evidence—"

"Circumstantial evidence. And just for the record, I've seen Max."

"When? Where?"

He turned for the door. "Wait for the grapevine to tell you."

"Don't do this, please." I went after him, caught his arm. "I'm not trying to condemn the boy without a trial."

"That's damn big of you, Frankie. In fact, you've condemned no one but yourself."

He slammed the door and headed for the car parked outside the garage.

"Where are you going?" I called after him, frantic at his attitude.

"To set a few lawmen straight," he said. "Don't wait up for me."

Those final words struck terror in my heart. I didn't know what was really going on, but whatever it was, I was drowning in it.

MY PHONE RANG not long after Johnny left. Hoping it was him, I jumped to answer.

"Hey," Joanie said, "I just heard."

"Heard what?"

"About Max spending the weekend in Kansas City with Johnny. As if you didn't know."

"Who told you that?"

"Lynda. She got it from her cousin, the cop."

"Oh, my God." I couldn't keep back my distress. Johnny had lied to the police for Max. When they found out, he'd be in more trouble than the boy would be.

"What did you say?"

"N-nothing."

"What I'm wondering is, why didn't you tell me Max was in the clear? There's been a lot of gossip circulating around out here today."

"I'm sorry."

"You did know, didn't you?"

"Joanie, I—I've gotta go." I hung up the phone without saying goodbye, and drove straight to the police station, my heart in my throat. Parking at the curb, I jumped out and ran inside. Looking around anxiously, I spotted Johnny in the chief's glass-fronted office.

Chief Brown waved me on in. He leaned back in his chair, his expression unreadable. "I was just fixin' to call you," he said, indicating an empty chair for me. "Not that I don't believe His Honor here, but it'll pacify the populace if I get some substantiation."

I glanced quickly at Johnny but he wouldn't meet my eyes. He was still angry, I realized. He probably thinks I won't back up whatever he's said.

Which I would, just as soon as I knew what it was.

"Whatever you want, Brownie." I sat down and clutched my hands in my lap.

"You're lookin' nervous, Frankie." He narrowed his eyes in speculation.

"What I'm looking is tired. What do you want from me?"

"First tell me why you come tearin' down here at this hour."

"I...I need to talk to my husband, that's all."

Brownie nodded. Johnny didn't move a muscle, didn't look at me.

"Tell me," Chief Brown said. "Has Johnny here been home the past couple of days?"

God, I hated to lie, and I wasn't very good at it, but for Johnny, I'd give it a try.

"That's right," I said, my chin rising in emphasis. "If that's all, why don't we go on home now, Johnny?"

Brownie laughed and turned to Johnny. "Your moll doesn't seem to have her story straight."

"Yeah," Johnny said, no humor at all on his face. "It's a damned good thing my father was home to verify my trip or you'd be throwing me in the clink about now."

I felt the knot in my stomach tighten, completely in the dark. "Johnny?" I said tentatively.

He ignored me, but Brownie said, "Okay, Frankie, now tell me the truth and I'll try to forget this little excursion into fiction."

"I don't know what you mean," I said haughtily, trying to brazen it out.

"Tell him the truth," Johnny snapped at me. "Unless you think I lied to you about going to Kansas City."

"I never suggested such a thing." I bit my lip, feeling myself falling into deep water.

"Hmm..." Brownie smiled. "So now you're agreeing that he wasn't in town all weekend, he was in Kansas City."

"Yes—no—I don't know. Whatever he said."

"Frankie," the cop said kindly, "when you find yourself in trouble, don't even *think* about trying to lie your way out. You got no talent for it."

At this point, I felt my temper rise. "What's going on here? Are you two just looking for ways to confuse me?" I demanded.

"Nah," Brownie said. "If you'll retract that first story about him being home all weekend, you can go."

"Then I retract," I said.

"Okay. You folks can go now. We got this all figured out."

Johnny and I walked out of the police station but he stayed ahead of me. Once we were on the sidewalk, he turned to look at me, a scowl on his face.

"If you think you made points with me by trying to lie to the chief, think again."

"I wasn't trying to make points. I was trying to help you!"

"You could have helped me by having a little faith."

"How could I, when I knew you were gone all weekend and couldn't possibly give Max an alibi?"

"You might have put two and two together and asked if anyone went with me."

I rocked back on my heels, all the breath knocked out of my body. "You mean—"

He nodded. "I took Max with me. I didn't plan it, it just happened. I saw him wandering around downtown and stopped to ask him if he'd like to come along with me. I called his mother but she was out of town so I got permission from his grandmother."

"His grandmother said he was out of town and I guess he was."

"You heard that on your grapevine, did you?"

"Don't start, Johnny. I feel bad enough as it is."

"Babe, you ain't seen nothin' yet."

My heart stopped beating and I stared at him.

He spoke very softly. "You said you'd trust me. You said you'd believe me. When I told you I knew for a fact that Max was innocent, you started making up lies to support me with the cops because you didn't believe a word I said."

"That's not fair!" I clenched my hands into fists. "If you'd been honest with me and said Max was with you—"

"Your mind was made up when I walked in the house. You didn't even ask for an explanation, you simply chose not to believe me."

"No, Johnny. That's not how it was."

He put his fingertips on my lips, stilling me. "I know how it was, and it was a deal breaker."

He turned and walked away from me while his words sank in.

I THOUGHT HE'D come back. Once he got over his anger, he'd realize that I hadn't done all that much. I'd apologize for *anything* at this point. Hell, I'd adopt Max if that would make Johnny happy.

I didn't hear from him for ten days and when he finally appeared, it was to tell me he'd decided divorce was the only solution.

"If you think I'll give you a divorce over this silly little squabble, you're living in dreamland," I yelled at him. "Johnny, I'm sorry! I'm sorry for everything. I'm sorry for not believing you and for suspecting Max and for lying to the police. What else can I say?"

"It doesn't matter what you say. You've worn me out, Frankie. It's got to the point where I can't trust you whether you trust me or not."

My shock knew no bounds. He had never turned on me this way. I wanted to scream and run out of the room but I knew that would be the end, for sure.

"We can work this out," I pleaded.

"Been there, done that. Remember the last time we got together at my place in Chicago? I asked just one thing of you—that you'd trust me. You obviously don't. At the time, we were talking about sex, but trust covers a whole lot more."

"I do trust you, Johnny. It's just that…I'm not perfect, no matter how hard I try. I make mistakes just like everybody else. You don't have to throw me overboard for one little screwup."

"You think it's only one?" He shook his head, looking dispirited. "We've hit the end of the road and this time it's for good. I'm going back to Chicago to take over for my father and—"

"What about Max?" I was desperate to slow him down. "Are you just going to walk out on him?"

"I've already talked to him. He knows I'm going, but he also knows I'll always be his friend. He won't be forgotten or overlooked."

"But I will," I said bitterly. "I couldn't be any more contrite than I am right now. Maybe in time, you'll get past this."

"We'll be divorced if and when that ever happens," he said.

"Don't be so sure." I straightened, my shoulders

going back. "If you think I'm going to let you walk away as easy as that, you've got another think coming."

"Meaning?"

"I'll fight this to the bitter end."

He shrugged and turned away as if he didn't give a damn. "Do what you have to," he said. "You'll be hearing from my lawyers."

He paused at the door. "They caught the kid who bombed the bank, you know."

"I hadn't heard."

"Grapevine down?"

I rose above his sarcasm. "Who was it?"

"A kid whose basketball team got beat by the Fair-weather Miners. One more thing… Do you know what today's date is?"

That was a surprise. "Sure. This is Thursday, May…fourteenth? 1998."

"Frank Sinatra died today."

He dug in his pocket and I knew what was in his hand before I saw it. He tossed the silver dollar through the air and it hit my arm and bounced to the floor.

"I think it's time to spend the damned thing," he said. "Either that or toss it away."

I threw my shoe at him as he walked out, but it only hit the door.

CHAPTER NINETEEN

I FOUGHT THE good fight, just as I told him I would, but after a while both my lawyer and I ran out of ways to avoid the inevitable. Johnny didn't get frustrated, didn't seem to care, but he didn't come home to me, either.

Then one day in 1999, he walked into Reva's Café and was promptly mobbed by the patrons.

"Johnny, long time no see…"

"Lookin' good, boy…"

"Really sorry to hear about you and Frankie…"

I watched all this, a glass in one hand and a towel in the other. Now what? I hadn't seen him in months so it must be important.

To me, he said, "Got a minute, Frankie?"

"Of course." I put down the glass I'd been polishing and gave him my attention.

"Let's sit down," he countered, leading the way to a table in the corner. Naturally I followed, as always.

Once we were seated, he said, "I've got something for you."

"Oh?" Now what? Maybe he'd reconsidered and brought me a gift. He seemed so cool and at ease that it might not be anything bad.

He reached into his briefcase and pulled out a sheaf

of papers. Laying them on the table, he said, "Congratulations. You're a free woman."

The divorce papers. I stared down at them, horrified, and took a shaky breath. "This is why you came here?"

"That's right."

"I thought it would come in the mail, or that I'd get a call from my lawyer."

"I volunteered to make the delivery," he said. "I wanted everything to be clean and clear."

"Are you kidding?"

"Relax," he said. "I'm glad it's over."

"I don't think so." I rose to my feet, my whole body trembling. "Stand up, *please.*"

He frowned, did as I asked. "What are you up to?"

"This." I put my arms around him and kissed him.

This was so not me. I hated audiences, and I hated people knowing my business, but if I didn't do something now, I'd be missing what was probably my last chance to make it up to him.

For a moment I thought he wouldn't respond. That moment passed, and he folded me into his embrace, his mouth hot and hard on mine. When he finally released me, I could barely stand.

His lips moved and I think he said, "Satisfied?" but couldn't be sure because everyone in Reva's Café was applauding.

I braced my hands on his chest. "I still love you." He couldn't hear me but I knew he understood what I said.

"Love's not enough anymore." He spoke directly into my ear.

"It is for me." I pushed hair away from my face and

tried to regain my composure. "I know you still love me, too. Let's tear up these papers and stop acting so silly."

"I bring you divorce papers and you propose at the same time?" He shook his head in amazement.

I leaned closer. "The divorce was your idea, not mine. I'm prepared to ignore it."

"Too late."

"Ah, Johnny," Ron put in from his booth nearby. "Everybody knows you two were made for each other. She's suffered long enough. Why don't you give her a break?"

"Yeah, a break!"

"Come on, Johnny."

"What do you want, blood?"

"I want to be friends." He reached out and shook my hand as if he'd met me five minutes ago.

I was sick of being a laughingstock in my own hometown, which should have given Johnny some idea of how determined I was. Anyone who'd marry and divorce the same man three times had to be serious or crazy to suggest a fourth try. Before I could try another approach, he spoke.

"Time for me to hit the road," he said. "Have a good life, Frankie."

Present, St. Louis

MEMORIAL HOSPITAL loomed ahead, overpowering the neighborhood above which it rose. Frankie could hardly believe it. After all this time, all these miles, she was just steps away from completing the most dangerous and emotional journey of her life.

She smiled wryly. It reminded her of a dying man whose life passed before him. Not a good omen.

She stopped in front of the hospital entryway, motor idling, and looked around the huge parking lot. An ice scraper passed by, accounting for what appeared to be decent footing. The rain and sleet had finally stopped and although the sky remained gray, she thought the storm was over.

Now she had only her own storm with which to deal.

For a few moments, she sat there in the car, hands on the steering wheel, thinking. How Johnny would respond to the sight of her she couldn't imagine but she'd make the trip again in a heartbeat.

But now it was time to face the inevitable. Driving carefully into the nearest empty space, she climbed stiffly out of the car. Slamming the door behind her, she hiked toward the hospital entrance on wobbly legs.

Soon, Frankie stood at the door to Johnny's room, afraid to go in and unable to turn away. Her entire body hurt from all those hours of driving in such horrible conditions. Everything she'd gone through seemed to land on her shoulders like the weight of an anvil. Emotions too near the surface threatened to break loose at any minute.

"You must be Mrs. Davis."

Frankie, deep in her own world, started. "Yes."

A young black nurse stepped forward, smiling. "I helped take care of Mr. Davis when he first came in."

"Thank you for that." Frankie frowned. "How did you know who I am?"

"He spoke to you in the emergency room. He was only half-conscious at the time but he kept saying the same thing."

Frankie held her breath. "Yes?"

"He said, 'I love you, Frankie.'"

The words stabbed deep into Frankie's heart. They had loved each other forever. Why had they spent so many of those years apart?

During the long drive, she'd finally realized that all that wasted time was because of her, not because of him. She'd made so many mistakes that it was a wonder he put up with her as long as he did.

The nurse's eyes widened. "Are you all right, Mrs. Davis? You look like you're about to pass out."

Frankie waved away help. "I'm fine, or I will be, as soon as I see Johnny. I'm just a little tired. Can I go in now?"

"Of course. If you need anything, call out." The nurse swung open the door and stepped aside. "I'll tell his doctor you're here."

Taking a deep breath, Frankie walked into the room of the prince she'd fought icy dragons to reach.

ALL FRANKIE SAW at first was a nurse leaning over the bed. She turned with a smile.

"Mrs. Davis?"

"Yes."

"I'm happy to tell you that Mr. Davis is with us again. He's doing remarkably well, all things considered. I'll get out of here and give you two some privacy."

"Thank you."

The nurse left the room. Slowly Frankie approached the bed and looked down, almost afraid of what she might see.

Johnny seemed at complete peace, lying there on

crisp white sheets with his eyes closed. He was a bit pale but still perfect, no injuries or bandages on his face. There was no breathing tube, thank God, just an IV and heart monitor leading to stands and machines beside the bed.

Love welled up in Frankie's chest and she bent to kiss him on the lips. Which moved beneath hers.

Johnny opened his eyes and whispered, "Frankie?"

Her heart stopped beating. "I prayed for this—that you'd be conscious by the time I got here."

"They…" He swallowed hard, as if his throat was dry. "They…they didn't tell me you were coming."

'I asked them not to. I was afraid you wouldn't see me.'

"You knew I would."

"I hoped." She sat in the chair beside the bed and put one hand on the curve of his elbow. Just the warmth of his flesh brought her pleasure. After a moment, she added, "We have so much to talk about. Are you up to it?"

"I think so. I'll try." He looked down at his body extended beneath the sheet. "I haven't come to grips with what's happened to me yet, Frankie. I have no idea what my future will be."

"Nobody knows what the future will be." She leaned forward, determined to tell him now. "Johnny, I have something to say, something I've put off for years, for decades—"

He wet his lips with his tongue. "This doesn't sound so good," he muttered.

"It isn't, but I want to make everything right."

"Frankie—" She heard a warning note in there

somewhere, as if he wasn't sure he wanted to hear what she had to say at all.

She longed to turn away, to ignore her part in their problems, but she wouldn't—not now. She opened her shoulder bag and reached for her wallet. Drawing out a wrinkled blue envelope, she asked him, "Can you read? I mean, is your vision all right?"

"So far as I know. It was my heart that gave out on me. What do you have there?"

"The missing letter, the letter Mother waylaid and you never got. I found it with her things after her death. I've carried it ever since, trying to get up the nerve to give it to you."

"That was a long time ago. What does the letter have to do with now?"

"Read it and you'll see." She pulled the single sheet from the envelope and handed it to him.

"My glasses…?"

She reached for the tortoiseshell pair lying on his bedside table. Handing them to him, she said, "You, too?"

"Only to read. You, too?"

She nodded. "Time's a bitch," she said, smiling.

He laughed and put on the glasses, then unfolded the letter. She knew how it started: *Johnny, I'm in trouble. I don't want to tell you this but I'm pregnant. I don't want to ruin your life or anything but I have to decide what to do—*

"My God. I can't believe this. I'd have come home instantly if I'd got this."

"That's what I hoped when I wrote it, but when I didn't hear anything from you—"

"Frankie, what did you do? Please say you didn't get an abortion?"

"No. I could never do that." Her head drooped unhappily. "I went to Tulsa and stayed with Aunt Eileen until the baby was born. Then—" She dragged in a deep breath. "I gave him up for adoption."

"Him…a boy?"

She nodded. "That's all I know about it, except that Aunt Eileen said he was going to a doctor and his wife in Wichita."

"How have you lived with this all these years?"

She flinched. "Did I make the wrong choice? I thought that was best because I was so young and you weren't with me. I don't see how I could have kept him—"

He groaned and reached for her hand. "That's not what I meant. I meant you must have gone through hell, giving him up and carrying that burden alone all this time. If only I'd known…"

"I've tried to tell you so many times, but I didn't think you could ever forgive me. I was…afraid."

He opened his arms and she leaned into them. Holding her, he said, "This explains why you were so pissed at me when I came home."

"I thought you knew about the baby but just didn't care."

His arms tightened around her, and simultaneously they said, "Can you ever forgive me?"

Nervous laughter followed and she straightened. "I forgave you long ago, once I finally accepted that you'd never seen the letter. Can you forgive me?"

"Yes!" He groaned. "How did we get in this mess,

Frankie? I know we've both made some bad moves. I know we've failed to trust each other when we should have but…"

"There's still time for us to get it right," she murmured.

"I don't know about that."

She squeezed his hand hard. "You can't forgive me for not trusting you? Although I actually did trust you, in my own way. It just came out all wrong."

"Everything's different now." The ease had left his voice.

"Different how?" Near panic, she wondered if indeed their time had passed.

"Different because I'm in this place and I don't really know how bad a mess I'm in." He gestured to the hospital room. "Different because we've tried and failed so many times. Different because we're still the same people and likely to make the same mistakes."

She leaned back so she could see him clearly. "We're who we are. Can't we live with that? Can't you live with my concern for—for propriety? I know I can live with your individualism and your do-gooder tendencies. Why do either one of us have to be perfect?"

"You can't fly in the face of history, Frankie."

"History." Her blood seemed to freeze in her veins. "Don't you get it? I don't care about what happened before, about who made what mistake. I want to start over. I'm asking right now—will you marry me again, Johnny?"

"Let me think," he said.

"My God, what do I have to do to convince you?"

He didn't reply, just lay there looking at her.

"All right," she said then, "how's this. We won't get

married until it feels right to you, but in the meantime, we'll live together."

"We'll what?"

She knew that would get his attention. "Live together," she announced, her voice strong and sure.

"Little Frankie Hale would never live with a man without benefit of clergy," he said. "Everyone would know and gossip about us. You're putting me on, right?"

"Wrong! You can go back home with me and we'll let people *think* we're married but we won't be. That means if you can't take it, you can leave without complications. Could there be a better deal than that?"

He let out a hoarse laugh. "If there is, I've never heard it. If you can take it, so can I."

She fell against his chest, kissing him, hugging him. Against her cheek, he murmured, "Do you think we can get him back?"

"Who?"

"Our son."

"Our son is in his forties! I don't know about getting him back."

"Maybe he has kids of his own. We'll get them back, too." The corner of his mouth tilted in a grin that slipped. "If we do that, people will know. Can you stand the talk?"

"I don't give a damn about the talk. I'm so surprised you want to find our son after all this time. I've always thought about him, wanted to know if he had a good life, to explain to him what happened."

"That's what we'll do. We'll find him together."

She kissed his throat. "Does this mean you'll marry me, or will we live in sin?"

"I'll marry you, but remember this—a fourth divorce would finish me off."

"It would finish both of us, so we won't do it." She pressed her hand against his cheek and looked into those beautiful blue eyes. "I've done a lot of thinking on this trip, a lot of remembering. I'm not afraid of what may come. Whatever it takes, we'll deal with. There's just one more thing, though."

"What now?"

"I'm going to give Reva's to Mindy and Jerry. She's earned it with all the support she's given me. Neither of our girls is interested so she'll keep it in the family. That way I can live in Chicago with you, or in Fairweather, or travel or whatever we want."

He looked astonished. "You'd give up the café?"

"I've already given it up in my heart. You're my top priority, honey."

He looked a little embarrassed. "In that case," he said, "you can tell the girls. I don't have the guts."

I reared back from him. "They already think we're crazy. There's not much chance I can convince them otherwise at this late date."

"Hey, we don't care what anybody thinks anymore. Remember?"

"I remember."

They laughed, and then she touched his lips lightly with her fingertips. "I brought Frank's silver dollar with me," she said. "I don't think we can blame it for all we've been through."

"We did beat Elvis and Priscilla's record, just like that other Frankie said. I guess it is good luck."

She nodded. "So is the carving you put on that tree the day we met—Frankie and Johnny."

"When we get home I'll add another word…forever."

"Forever," she agreed, her heart swelling with love and relief. "Kiss me, Johnny. Kiss me…."

* * * * *

Silhouette Desire kicks off 2009 with
MAN OF THE MONTH, *a yearlong program
featuring incredible heroes by stellar authors.*

When Navy SEAL Hunter Cabot returns home
for some much-needed R & R, he discovers he's
a married man. There's just one problem: he's
never met his "bride."

Enjoy this sneak peek at Maureen Child's
AN OFFICER AND A MILLIONAIRE.
Available January 2009 from Silhouette Desire.

One

Hunter Cabot, Navy SEAL, had a healing bullet wound in his side, thirty days' leave and, apparently, a wife he'd never met.

On the drive into his hometown of Springville, California, he stopped for gas at Charlie Evans's service station. That's where the trouble started.

"Hunter! Man, it's good to see you! Margie didn't tell us you were coming home."

"Margie?" Hunter leaned back against the front fender of his black pickup truck and winced as his side gave a small twinge of pain. Silently then, he watched as the man he'd known since high school filled his tank.

Charlie grinned, shook his head and pumped gas. "Guess your wife was lookin' for a little 'alone' time with you, huh?"

"My—" Hunter couldn't even say the word. *Wife?* He didn't have a wife. "Look, Charlie…"

"Don't blame her, of course," his friend said with a wink as he finished up and put the gas cap back on. "You being gone all the time with the SEALs must be hard on the ol' love life."

He'd never had any complaints, Hunter thought,

frowning at the man still talking a mile a minute. "What're you—"

"Bet Margie's anxious to see you. She told us all about that R & R trip you two took to Bali." Charlie's dark brown eyebrows lifted and wiggled.

"Charlie…"

"Hey, it's okay, you don't have to say a thing, man."

What the hell could he say? Hunter shook his head, paid for his gas and as he left, told himself Charlie was just losing it. Maybe the guy had been smelling gas fumes too long.

But as it turned out, it wasn't just Charlie. Stopped at a red light on Main Street, Hunter glanced out his window to smile at Mrs. Harker, his second-grade teacher who was now at least a hundred years old. In the middle of the crosswalk, the old lady stopped and shouted, "Hunter Cabot, you've got yourself a wonderful wife. I hope you appreciate her."

Scowling now, he only nodded at the old woman—the only teacher who'd ever scared the crap out of him. What the hell was going on here? Was everyone but him nuts?

His temper beginning to boil, he put up with a few more comments about his "wife" on the drive through town before finally pulling into the wide, circular drive leading to the Cabot mansion. Hunter didn't have a clue what was going on, but he planned to get to the bottom of it. Fast.

He grabbed his duffel bag, stalked into the house and paid no attention to the housekeeper, who ran at him, fluttering both hands. "Mr. Hunter!"

"Sorry, Sophie," he called out over his shoulder as he took the stairs two at a time. "Need a shower, then we'll talk."

He marched down the long, carpeted hallway to the rooms that were always kept ready for him. In his suite, Hunter tossed the duffel down and stopped dead. The shower in his bathroom was running. His *wife?*

Anger and curiosity boiled in his gut, creating a churning mass that had him moving forward without even thinking about it. He opened the bathroom door to a wall of steam and the sound of a woman singing— off-key. Margie, no doubt.

Well, if she was his wife… Hunter walked across the room, yanked the shower door open and stared in at a curvy, naked, temptingly wet woman.

She whirled to face him, slapping her arms across her naked body while she gave a short, terrified scream.

Hunter smiled. "Hi, honey. I'm home."

* * * * *

Be sure to look for
AN OFFICER AND A MILLIONAIRE
by USA TODAY *bestselling author Maureen Child.*
Available January 2009 from Silhouette Desire.

CELEBRATE
60 YEARS
OF PURE READING PLEASURE
WITH HARLEQUIN®!

**We'll be spotlighting a different series
every month throughout 2009
to celebrate our 60th anniversary.
Look for Silhouette Desire® in January!**

Collect all 12 books in the Silhouette Desire®
Man of the Month continuity, starting in
January 2009 with *An Officer and a Millionaire*
by *USA TODAY* bestselling author
Maureen Child.

*Look for one new Man of the Month title
every month in 2009!*

REQUEST YOUR FREE BOOKS!
2 FREE NOVELS PLUS 2 FREE GIFTS!

HARLEQUIN®

Super Romance®

Exciting, emotional, unexpected!

YES! Please send me 2 FREE Harlequin Superromance® novels and my 2 FREE gifts (gifts are worth about $10). After receiving them, if I don't wish to receive any more books, I can return the shipping statement marked "cancel." If I don't cancel, I will receive 6 brand-new novels every month and be billed just $4.69 per book in the U.S. or $5.24 per book in Canada, plus 25¢ shipping and handling per book and applicable taxes, if any*. That's a savings of close to 15% off the cover price! I understand that accepting the 2 free books and gifts places me under no obligation to buy anything. I can always return a shipment and cancel at any time. Even if I never buy another book from Harlequin, the two free books and gifts are mine to keep forever.

135 HDN EEX7 336 HDN EEYK

Name	(PLEASE PRINT)	
Address		Apt. #
City	State/Prov.	Zip/Postal Code

Signature (if under 18, a parent or guardian must sign)

Mail to the Harlequin Reader Service:
IN U.S.A.: P.O. Box 1867, Buffalo, NY 14240-1867
IN CANADA: P.O. Box 609, Fort Erie, Ontario L2A 5X3

Not valid to current subscribers of Harlequin Superromance books.

Want to try two free books from another line?
Call 1-800-873-8635 or visit www.morefreebooks.com.

* Terms and prices subject to change without notice. N.Y. residents add applicable sales tax. Canadian residents will be charged applicable provincial taxes and GST. Offer not valid in Quebec. This offer is limited to one order per household. All orders subject to approval. Credit or debit balances in a customer's account(s) may be offset by any other outstanding balance owed by or to the customer. Please allow 4 to 6 weeks for delivery. Offer available while quantities last.

Your Privacy: Harlequin is committed to protecting your privacy. Our Privacy Policy is available online at www.eHarlequin.com or upon request from the Reader Service. From time to time we make our lists of customers available to reputable third parties who may have a product or service of interest to you. If you would prefer we not share your name and address, please check here. ☐

HSR08R

USA TODAY BESTSELLING AUTHOR

TARA
TAYLOR
QUINN

A woman, a judge—a target

Criminal court judge Hannah Montgomery is presiding over a
murder trial. When the jury finds the defendant, Bobby Donahue,
not guilty, Hannah's convinced they've reached the wrong verdict.
Especially when strange things start happening around her...

AT CLOSE
RANGE

*Available the first week
of December 2008,
wherever paperbacks
are sold!*

"An exceptionally powerful book."
—*Booklist* on *Behind Closed Doors*

Silhouette
SPECIAL EDITION™

USA TODAY bestselling author
MARIE FERRARELLA

FORTUNES OF TEXAS: RETURN TO RED ROCK

PLAIN JANE AND THE PLAYBOY

To kill time at a New Year's party, playboy Jorge Mendoza shows the host's teenage son how to woo the ladies. The random target of Jorge's charms: wallflower Jane Gilliam. But with one kiss at midnight, introverted Jane turns the tables on this would-be Casanova, as the commitment-phobe falls for her hook, line and sinker!

Available January 2009
wherever you buy books.

HARLEQUIN

Super Romance

COMING NEXT MONTH

#1536 A FOREVER FAMILY • Jamie Sobrato
Going Back

He's not part of her plans. So why can't single mom Emmy Van Amsted stop thinking about her college sweetheart Aidan Caldwell? She's returned to this town to start over, not revisit history. Still, Aidan's presence is making her rethink her plans.

#1537 THE SECRET SHE KEPT • Amy Knupp
A Little Secret

Jake had blown out of town so fast—and so angry at his dad—Savannah Salinger had no clue how to find him, let alone tell him she was pregnant. And she's kept her secret for so long...what's she going to do now that Jake Barnes is back?

#1538 A MAN SHE COULDN'T FORGET • Kathryn Shay

Clare Boneil has stepped into a life she can't remember. That's especially so for the two men pursuing her. She cares for both, but only one makes her feel alive, feel like herself. Until her memory returns, can she trust her heart to lead her to the one she loves?

#1539 THE GROOM CAME BACK • Abby Gaines
Marriage of Inconvenience

It's past time Dr. Jack Mitchell divorced Callie Summers. Rumors of their marriage are beginning to affect his reputation as a star neurosurgeon—not to mention his love life. But returning home for the first time in years, Jack doesn't even recognize the knockout woman she's become. And she's not letting him leave home again without a fight.

#1540 DADDY BY SURPRISE • Debra Salonen
Spotlight on Sentinel Pass

Jackson Treadwell is proving he's got a wild side. Clad in leather astride his motorcycle, wild he is. He so doesn't expect to meet a woman who makes him want to settle down—let alone settle with kids! But he's never met anyone as persuasive as Kat Petroski.

#1541 PICTURES OF US • Amy Garvey
Everlasting Love

The photographs that line the mantel of the Butterfield home celebrate every highlight of Michael and Tess's life together—from sweethearts to marriage to parenthood. But when crisis strikes, can these same images guide them back to each other?